U0088260

附 MP3

用你會的單字說英文

陳久娟★編著

Speak English

國家圖書館出版品預行編目資料

用你會的單字說英文／陳久娟編著.
--初版. ---臺北縣汐止市：雅典文化, 民97.12
　　面；公分. --（英語工具書系列：5）
　　ISBN：978-986-7041-68-5 (平裝附光碟片)

　1. 英語　　　　　　2. 會話
805.188　　　　　　　　　　　　　97018534

英語工具書系列：5

用你會的單字說英文

編　　著◎陳久娟

出 版 者◎雅典文化事業有限公司

登 記 證◎局版北市業字第五七○號

發 行 人◎黃玉雲

執行編輯◎林美娟

編 輯 部◎221 台北縣汐止市大同路三段 194-1 號 9 樓

電　　話◎02-86473663　傳真◎02-86473660

郵　　撥◎18965580 雅典文化事業有限公司

法律顧問◎永信法律事務所　林永頌律師

總 經 銷◎永續圖書有限公司

　　　　　221 台北縣汐止市大同路三段 194-1 號 9 樓

　　　　　EmailAdd: yungjiuh@ms45.hinet.net

　　　　　網站◎ www.foreverbooks.com.tw

　　　　　郵撥◎ 18669219

　　　　　電話◎ 02-86473663　傳真◎ 02-86473660

初　　版◎2008 年 12 月

定　　價◎ NT$ 280 元

序

　　每個人會的英文單字，基本上絕對有 500-1000 字，你只要按照本書的內容，循序漸進的學習，從開場白、問候語、自我介紹、詢問、聊天、表達喜怒哀樂到説拜拜，就學英文入門而言，先利用你會的有限單字來正確的組合，在適當的時機使用，這樣一來你就可以和外國人開口説英文了，那你也成功的踏出英語會話學習的第一步了。當然了，對話中會需要許多單字去表達你的意思，如何增加新單字就要看個人進修功力了。本書將用最簡單的單字，最簡單的會話讓你輕鬆開口説英文。

Chapter 1 最基本的第一句話

相信這第一句話大家都會說了

Chapter 2 最重要的第二句話

How are you? 之後常常不知說什麼……

Chapter 3 打開話匣子

溝通最重要的就是找到話題

Chapter 4 客套話

讚美是送給朋友最好的禮物

Chapter 5 形容喜怒哀樂的句子

對話中不可缺少形容感覺的句子

Chapter 6 聊天-食衣住

談話中最基本的生活面

Chapter 7 聊天-行育樂

最常遇到的狀況與情境

Chapter 8 聊天-生活

遇到這些狀況時要會說

Chapter 9 道別語

該說再見了

Chapter 1

最基本的第一句話

相信這第一句話大家都會說了

開場白/問候語

▶嗨！

Hi!

Hello!

▶你好嗎？

How are you?

▶你好。

How do you do.

▶今天過的如何？

How's your day?

▶早安！

Good morning!

▶午安！

Good Afternoon!

▶晚安

你(們)好(指傍晚到晚上的時間)

Good evening!

▶晚安！

Good night!

▶近來如何？
　一切都還好嗎？

> Is everything ok?
> How's everything?

▶最近有什麼新鮮事嗎？

> What's new?
> What's up?
> How's it going?
> What's happening?

回應問候語

▶謝謝你，我很好。

> Fine. Thank you.

　注：多半是對方問 how are you 時的回答。

▶還不壞。

> Not bad.
> I can't complain!

▶沒啥好抱怨的！

> I have nothing to complain about!

▶一切都好。

> Everything is fine.

▶好久沒有你的消息了！

好久不見！

> It's been a while!
>
> Long time no see!
>
> I haven't heard from you for a long time!

▶很高興能聽到你的聲音。

> I'm glad to hear your voice.

▶沒什麼。

> Nothing special.
>
> Nothing much.

> └ 註：多半用來回答熟朋友間的隨口問候。

▶很好啊！

> Great!
>
> I'm great!

▶噢，還好啦！

> Well, so so.
>
> Well, ok.

▶還好吧！我想。

> Okay. I guess.
>
> Fine. I suppose.

▶很忙！

> Busy!
>
> Very busy!

Chapter 2

最重要的第二句話

How are you? 之後常常不知說什麼……

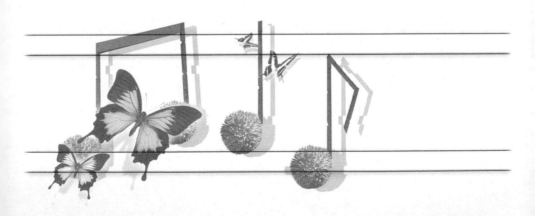

當你聽不清楚時(一定要會的第二句話)

▶抱歉。請再說一次(好嗎？)

> Pardon?
> Excuse me?
> Say again?
> I am sorry?
> Say what?
> Come again?
> What?

▶能不能請你再重複一次？

> Can you repeat again?
> Can you say that again?

▶請你說慢一點？

> Could you speak slower, please?

▶我聽不見。

> I can't hear you.

▶你剛剛說什麼？

> What did you just say?

▶ 我不太懂。

> I don't understand.

▶請您大聲一點好嗎？

> Would you speak a little bit louder, please?

自我介紹/介紹認識

▶請介紹一下你自己。

Tell me about yourself.
Talk about yourself!
Introduce yourself briefly, please.

▶我叫 David。

My name is David.
I am David.

▶你叫什麼名字？

What is your name?
May I have your name?

▶很高興認識你。

Nice to meet you.
Nice meeting you.
Pleasure to meet you.

▶我很榮幸(認識你)。

My pleasure.
It's my pleasure.

▶我跟朋友一起來的。

I came here with my friend.

▶我是 John，James 的老朋友。我們認識很久了。

I am John. James' old friend, we go way back.

個人資料

▶我朋友都叫我 J.

My friends used to call me J.

▶叫我 J 就好了。

Just call me J.

▶我今年30歲。

I am 30 years old.

▶我是1973年10月10日生。

I was born on nineteen seventy-three(1973), Octor tenth (10/10).

▶我幾乎快190公分高。

I am almost 190 centimeters.

▶我體重62公斤。

I am 62 kilograms.

血型

▶你是什麼血型？

What's your blood type?

▶我血型 O 型。

I am type O.
I am an O.

星座

▶你的星座是什麼？

What's your sign?

▶我是天蠍座的人。

I am a Scorpio.
I belong to Scorpio.

VOCABULARY
星座單字

Aries	白羊座，白羊座的人		
Taurus	金牛座，金牛座的人		
Gemini	雙子座，雙子座的人		
Cancer	巨蟹座，巨蟹座的人		
Leo	獅子座，獅子座的人		
Virgo	處女座，處女座的人		
Aquarius	水瓶座，水瓶座的人		
Capricorn	魔羯座，魔羯座的人		
Sagittarius	人馬座，射手座	Sagittarian	出身射手座的人
Piscean	出身雙魚座的人	Libran	出身天秤座的人
Pisces	雙魚座	Libra	天秤座
Scorpion	出身天蠍座的人	Scorpio	天蠍座

生肖

▶你屬什麼？

What animal sign were you born under?
What's your animal sign?
What's your Chinese horoscope?

▶我是龍年出生的。

I was born under the year of dragon.

▶2008年是中國鼠年。

The year 2008 is the Chinese year of rat.

VOCABULARY
生肖單字

rat	鼠	ox	牛
tiger	虎	rabbit	兔
dragon	龍	snake	蛇
horse	馬	sheep	羊
lamb	羊	monkey	猴
rooster	雞	chicken	雞
dog	狗	pig	豬
boar	豬	Chinese astrology 中國星象	

介紹朋友給他人

▶Larry，這是 John！

Larry, this is John!

▶我可以帶個朋友來嗎？

May I bring a friend?

▶可以帶朋友來嗎？

May I bring my friend along?

▶我可以帶朋友來嗎？

Can I take a friend?

生長背景，居住環境

▶我來自台北。

I come from Taipei.

▶我在台北出生。

I was born in Taipei.

▶我在台北出生長大。

I was born and raised in Taipei.

▶我來自一個小鎮。

I am from a small town.

▶我在一個農場長大。

I was brought up in a farm.

家庭狀況

▶你有幾個小孩？

How many children do you have?

▶你家裡有多少成員？

How many people are there in your family?

▶我有個七歲的兒子/女兒

I have a 7-year-old boy/girl.

▶我有兩個小孩。

I have two kids.

▶我有兩個哥哥(或弟弟)和一個姐姐(或妹妹)。

I have two brothers and a sister.

▶我和父母同住。

My parents and I live together.

▶我自己一個人住。

I live alone.

▶我跟朋友合住一間屋子。

I share a house with my friends.

▶我的家人感情很親密。

My family are very close.

▶我來自一個大家庭。

I come from a big family.

VOCABULARY
親屬稱謂

father	父親
mother	母親
husband	丈夫
wife	妻子
child / children	小孩子 / 小孩子(複數)
daughter	女兒
son	兒子
brother	兄弟
sister	姊妹
elder / younger brother	哥哥 / 弟弟
elder / younger sister	妹妹 / 姊姊
uncle	伯 / 叔 / 舅 / 姑 / 姨父
aunt	伯 / 叔 / 舅 / 姑 / 姨母
cousin	堂表兄弟姊妹
nephew	侄子
niece	侄女
father-in-law	公公
mother-in-law	婆婆
sister-in-law	嫂子 / 弟妹
brother-in-law	姊夫 / 妹夫
in-laws	姻親(尤指岳父母或公婆)

修習課程/求學過程

▶我主修企管。

My major is Business Administration.

▶我主修中國文學及法語。

I major in Chinese literature and French.

▶英文是必修課。

English is mandatory.
English is a mandatory course.
English is required.

▶我選修過日文。

I took Japanese.

▶我去過美國暑期英文遊學。

I went to US for a summer to study English.

▶我從沒出國唸過書。

I've never studied abroad.

▶我十歲時被轉到另一家學校。

When I was 10, I was transferred to another school.

▶因為我父母工作的關係，我經常轉學。

Because of my parent's job, I was transferring from school to school.

▶我在家自學。

I am home schooled.

▶我高中畢業後選擇了軍旅生涯。

After I graduating from high school, I chose a military career.

▶我服完兵役後，決定再度回到學校唸書。

After I finished my military service, I decided to go back to school again.

▶大學畢業後，我工作了兩年。

After graduating from college, I worked for 2 years.

▶我自費唸書。

I studied at my own expense.

▶我是半工半讀的學生。

I was in the work-study program.

▶我有雙主修學士學位。

I received a double-major bachelor's degree.

▶我正在修英語和中文學位。

I am working on my double major in English and Chinese.

▶我有雙學士學位。

I have a double degree.

└ 註：也可以用 dual gegree, combined degree.

└ 註：完成雙學位，表示在畢業時將獲得兩張畢業證書。

表明自己是誰介紹的

▶我是 Kevin 工作上的朋友。

I am a friend of Kevin's from his work.

▶我是 Kevin 的一個朋友。

I am a friend of Kevin's.

▶我跟 Kevin 一起來的。

I was here with Johnson.
I came with Johnson.

▶是 James 介紹我給 Mr. Woods 的。

It's James who introduced me to Mr. Woods.

▶James 介紹我來這裡的。

James introduced me here.

▶我看到電視上的廣告(而來的)。

I saw the TV ads.

▶我一年前和朋友來過。

I was here with a friend a year ago.

Chapter 3

打開話匣子

溝通最重要的就是找到話題

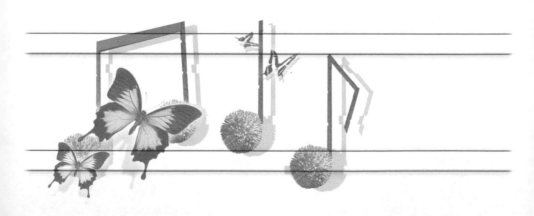

找尋共同點

▶你怎麼認識 James 的？

How do you know James?

▶你也是 Johnson 的朋友啊？

Are you a friend of Johnson, too?

▶你怎麼會來呢？/什麼風把你吹來的？

What brings you here?

Why are you here?

▶你也常來這裡嗎？

Do you come here often, too?

與對方相關的話題

▶你跟家人一起來的嗎？

Are you here with your family?

▶你是為了出差而來這裡的嗎？

Are you here for business?

▶你是哪裡人？

Where are you from?

▶你的工作是什麼？

What do you do?

▶你什麼時候到的？

When did you arrive?

引導對方發表意見或評論

▶電影滿好看的，你覺得呢？(電影發表會上)

　Great movie, isn't it?

▶電影真難看，對吧？

　The movie sucks, right?

▶甜點還不錯，對吧？(茶會或聚餐場合)

　Nice dessert, right?

▶真是不錯吧？

　Isn't it nice?

▶你喜歡這個表演嗎？

　Did you enjoy the show?

▶你覺得這部電影如何？

　How do you think about the movie?

▶你覺得這部電影的結局如何？

　How do you feel about the ending?

▶你喜歡哪個款式？(在時尚發表會上)

　Which styling do you prefer?

▶如果是你，你會怎麼做？

　What would you do if it were you?

請求幫助

▶請幫助我。

Please help me.
Could you do me a favor?
Please give me a hand.
I need a favor.

▶我想問點事情?

May I ask something?

▶你有空嗎?借用一分鐘好嗎?

Do you have a minute?
Can I have a minute?
Can you spare a minute for me?

▶我可以跟你談談嗎?

Can I talk to you?
Can I have a word with you?
May I have a word with you?

▶我可以私下跟你談話嗎?

Could I have a word with you privately?

▶我們該談一談!

We need to talk!
We should talk it over.
We should have a conversation.

緊急事件

▶我很急。

I am in a hurry.

▶這很急！

This is urgent!
This is rush!

▶這非常重要。

It is important.

▶儘快。

As soon as possible.

▶快一點！

Hurry up!
Speed up!
Faster!
Quicker!

▶趕一下進度。

Rush it!

其他

▶天氣不錯，可不是嗎？

Nice weather, isn't it?

▶天氣真糟！

真討厭！

真糟糕！

It sucks!

└ 註：藉由雙方共同經歷的壞天氣或其它很糟的狀況開啟談話，建立同
仇敵愾的同理心。

▶我以為你有個弟弟！

I thought you have a brother!

└ 註：故意以不相干的事情攀談。

▶我們見過面嗎？

Have we met?

Have we met before?

▶你昨天也有來這裡嗎？

Were you here last night?

▶你的眼睛很漂亮。

You have beautiful eyes.

▶我喜歡你的穿著。

I like your outfit.

Chapter 4

客套話

讚美是送給朋友最好的禮物

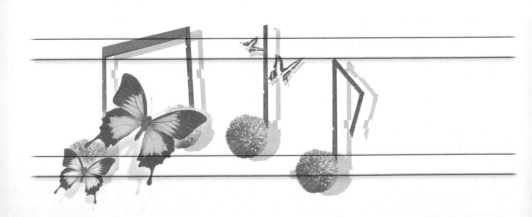

第二次見面

▶好久不見！

Long time no see!

▶好久沒有你的消息了！

I haven't heard from you for a long time!

▶近來如何？

How've you been?/How's it going?

▶很高興能聽到你的聲音。

I'm glad to hear your voice.

讚美

▶太棒了！

Wonderful!
Excellent!
Amazing.
Terrific!
Fantastic!
Marvelous!

▶酷！

Cool!
Neat!
This is cool!
This is neat!

►太棒了！

Great!
Good!
Awesome!
This is great!
Way to go!
This is awesome!
Super!

►難以置信！

Incredible!
That's incredible!

►真是壯麗。真厲害。

Spectacular.
Splendid.

►幹得好。

Well done.
Good job.
Nice job.
Wonderful job.
Good for you!
Way to go!

►我以你為榮！

I'm proud of you!

►你真厲害！

You're on top of it!

►不錯！

Not bad!

►了不起！

Remarkable!

►出類拔萃！

Outstanding!

►你今天看上去很棒。

You look great today.

►你今天真帥。

You look smart today.

└註：用來讚美男生的穿著正式挺拔。

►她品味很好。

She has very good taste.

►你的個性很好。

You have a very good personality.

►你今天看起來真迷人。

You look so charming today.

►他很有魅力。
他很迷人。

He is attractive.
He is charming.

▶她很美。

She is pretty.
She is beautiful.

▶她很可愛。

She is cute.

▶她很有幽默感。

She has a good sense of humor.

▶她很風趣。

She is funny.

▶你今天看起來真有精神。

You look sharp today.

▶我們為你感到驕傲。

We are proud of you.

▶保持好水準！

Keep up the good work!

▶這很傑出！

This is outstanding!

▶這再好不過了。

It can't be better!

鼓勵

▶要有耐性

Be patient.

▶不要放棄！

Don't give up!

▶你可以做得更好！

You can do better!

▶別氣餒！

Don't be frustrated!

▶放輕鬆！

Relax!

Take it easy!

▶那沒關係的！

It's no big deal!

▶你做得到的。

You can do that.

▶加油！

Go get it, tiger!

▶振作點！

Cheer up!

安慰

▶別擔心！
Don't worry!

▶那不是你的錯。
It's not your fault.

▶你盡力了！
You have done your best!

▶不會有事的！
You will be fine!

謙虛

▶你也很棒！
You are great, too.

▶那是我的榮幸。
It is my pleasure.

▶謝謝你的恭維。
I will take it as a compliment.

▶你說話總是很得體。
You always know the right thing to say.

形容正面性格

▶他的個性很好。

He is nice.

▶他非常實際。

He's very down-to-earth.

▶他很獨立。

He is independent.

▶他很有活力。/他精力旺盛。/他很活潑。

He is very energetic.

He is very active.

▶她是一個樂觀的人。

She is a cheerful girl.

She is an optimistic person.

└ 註：相反詞就是 pessimistic.

▶我很開明。/我頗能接受各種思想。

I am pretty open-minded.

▶她很有創意。

She is very creative.

▶她很外向。/她很善交際。

She is very outgoing.

She is a sociable girl.

▶她很友善。

She is very friendly.

▶她很受歡迎。

She is popular.

▶她很有趣/幽默。

She is a funny person.

▶我很好相處/隨和。

I am an easy going person.

▶他很值得信賴。

He is trustworthy.
He is reliable.
He is dependable.

▶他很誠實。

He is very honest.

▶他很真誠。

He is very sincere.
He is very genuine.

▶我很直率。

I am a straightforward person.

▶他很正直。

He is an upright person.
He is decent.

▶他很聰明。

He is smart/clever.

▶他很有天份。

He is talented/gifted.

▶他是天才。

He is a genius.

▶他反應很快。

He is very quick.
He is fast.

▶他是很熱誠的人。

He is an enthusiastic person.

▶他很熱情。

He is a warm person.
He is a very passionate person.

▶他很溫文/斯文。

He is gentle.

▶他斯文有禮。

He is gentle and polite.

▶他對人謙恭有禮。

He is courteous to everyone.

▶他很謙虛。

He is modest.

▶他很仁慈。/他很慈悲。/他很有同情心。

He is very kind

He is kind-hearted.

He is caring.

He is compassionate.

▶他很慷慨/大方。

He is generous.

▶她是一個勇敢的小女孩。

She is a brave little girl.

▶她是一位很有決心的女人。

She is a very determined woman.

▶他對自己很有信心。

He is very confident.

▶他(對生活)的態度很正面。

He has a positive attitude.

▶他很體貼。

He is very tender/considerate.

▶他很通情達理。

He is very understanding.

▶他很勤勞。

He is a diligent person.

He is a hardworking person.

▶他很專注。

He is dedicated.

▶他很有耐心。

He is a patient person.

He is patient with everyone.

▶他個性很有責任感。

He is very responsible.

形容負面性格

▶他很糟。

He is awful.

└ 註：一般形容「不好」都可以用這個字。

▶他很冷漠。

He is cold.

▶他個性懶惰。

He is lazy.

▶他個性傲慢。

He is arrogant.

▶我一定太容易相信人了。

I must be too trustful.

▶他個性膚淺。

He is shallow.

▶他的心地不好/卑鄙。

He is mean.

▶他很惡毒。

He is vicious.

▶他個性不友善。

He is unfriendly.

▶他個性多疑。

He is suspicious of everything.

▶他不誠實/不真誠。

He is dishonest.
He is insincere.
He is a liar.

▶他個性虛偽。

He is hypocritical.

▶他個性悲觀。

He is pessimistic.

└ 註：相反詞就是 optimistic.

▶他個性自私。

He is selfish.

▶她喜怒無常。/她很情緒化。

She is moody.

She is emotional.

▶她脾氣不好。

She has a bad temper.

She loses her temper easily.

▶他個性頑固。

He is stubborn.

He is headstrong.

▶他個性幼稚。/他不夠成熟。

He is immature.

▶他個性很愛指使人。

He is bossy.

▶他很愛批判人。/他總是不客觀地批判人。

He is judgmental.

▶她反應慢。

She is slow.

▶他笨笨的。

He is headless.

He is stupid.

▶他不太耐煩。

He is impatient.

▶他個性小氣/吝嗇。

> He is cheap.
> He is stingy.
> He is miserly.

▶他很勢利。/他很自大。

> He is snobbish.

▶他很貪心。

> He is greedy.

▶他很愛講話。

> He is talkative.

▶他愛爭辯。

> He is argumentative.

▶他很吵雜/喧噪。

> He is noisy.
> He is loud.

▶他個性衝動。

> He is impulsive.

▶她佔有慾太強了。

> She is too possessive.

▶她控制慾很強。

> She is very dominant.
> She is a control freak.

▶她愛吃醋。

> She is very jealousy.

▶她很愛現。

She is showy.

▶她很好管閒事。她很八卦。

She is nosy.

▶她很愛拍馬屁。

She is a brown noser.

▶她很粗野無理。

She is rude.

▶這很冒犯人。

This is offensive.

形容其他性格

▶他很敏感。

He is very sensitive.

▶他很多愁善感。

He is sentimental.

▶他個性內向。/他個性害羞。

He is shy.

▶她對任何事都很好奇。

She is curious about everything.

▶她很嚴格。

She is very strict.

►他很世故。/他很靈活。/他很伶俐。

He is sophisticated.

►他要求很高。

He is demanding.

►他野心勃勃。

He is ambitious.

►他有衝勁。

He is aggressive.

►她是無知的。

She is innocent.

►她個性天真/孩子氣。

She is naive.
She is childish.

►他個性保守。/他個性傳統。

He is conventional.
He is traditional.
He is a reserved person.
He is conservative.

►他是很拘謹的人。/他是很嚴謹的人。

He is a restrained person.

►他是一個精明的生意人。

He is a sharp business man.

▶他做事很小心謹慎。

He is a careful person.
He is very cautious.

▶他不適任此項工作。

He is incapable of this job.
He is incompetent of this job.

▶他適任這份工作。

He is qualified to do this job.

道謝

▶謝謝！

Thanks!
Thank you very much.

▶謝謝你的幫助。

Thank you for your help.

▶我很感激。

I appreciate it.
I am grateful!

▶不客氣。

Sure!
You are welcome.

▶我的榮幸！

My pleasure!

▶沒問題啦！

No problem.
Anytime!

▶我很高興你喜歡！

I am glad you like it.

▶我很高興聽到你這麼說。

Glad to hear that.

拒絕

▶不要這樣！/請停止！

Please stop!
Stop immediately!

▶不要就是不要。

No means no!

▶不要再說那個字了。

Don't say that again.

▶不要說黃色笑話。

Don't tell dirty jokes.

└ 註：crack jokes. 說笑話

▶不要說髒話。

　Don't speak dirty words.

▶這樣很不適當。

　This is unacceptable.
　It's inappropriate.
　It's not a proper thing to say.

▶這是（性）騷擾。

　This is (sexual) harassment

▶我不喜歡你剛剛說的話。

　I don't appreciate what you have just said.

▶這樣很冒犯(對方)。

　This is offensive.

▶這樣(的行為)很不適當。

　That is not proper.
　This is not a proper behavior.

▶請注意你的行為。

　Please behave.
　Please mind your manners.

▶你(說的話)令我很不舒服。

　It makes me uncomfortable.

▶說話請禮貌一點。

　Speak politely, please.

▶請放尊重一點。

Please show more respect.
Please show some respect.

▶我要尖叫囉！

I am going to scream.

└註：尤其是女性或小孩在公共場合碰到騷擾時可以說這句話。

▶這是(我最後一次)警告。

I'm warning you.
This is a warning.

└註：在拒絕後，對方仍再犯的情況下說這句話。

要求道歉/道歉語，以及回應

▶請為你的行為道歉。

Please apologize for your behavior.

▶請收回你說的話

Please take it back.

▶不好意思。/抱歉。/借過。

Excuse me.

▶對不起。/我很遺憾。

I am sorry.

▶我道歉。

My apology.

▶請原諒我。

Please excuse me./Please accept my apology.

▶我不是故意的。

I didn't mean it.

▶我該向你道歉。

I owe you an apology.

▶我真的很抱歉。

I am terribly sorry about it.

▶我想補償你。

I want to make it up to you.
I want to make it right for you.

▶沒關係。

Forget it./It's alright./I am ok with it.

▶別放在心上。

Never mind./Don't worry about that.

▶換成我可能也會這樣做。

I could have done the same thing.

▶我完全了解。

I completely understand.

▶我現在沒辦法討論這件事。

I can't discuss it right now.

└註：無法原諒對方，但又不願引發衝突的情況下。

Chapter 5

形容喜怒哀樂的句子

對話中不可缺少形容感覺的句子

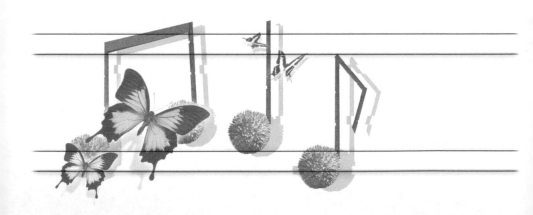

一般口語

▶真刺激。

Exciting.

▶我好難過。

I feel awful.

I feel terrible.

I feel horrible.

▶這好奇怪。

This is strange

This is weird.

This is unusual.

▶這令人覺得不舒服。

This is unpleasant!

▶答對了。

Bingo.

▶我無意冒犯。

No offense.

▶別生氣。

No hard feelings.

▶那麼，沒事囉？

So, are we fine?

└註：吵架之後合好所說的話。

▶我也這樣認為。

I think so.

▶你說的對！

That's right!

▶聽起來不錯。

Sounds good!
Sounds interesting!

▶這一言難盡/這說來話長。

It's a long story.

▶現在不是一個好時機。

It's not a good time.

▶我別無選擇。

I have no choice.

▶這不關我的事/這我不管。

I don't care.

▶那不是我的錯。

It wasn't my fault.

▶我已經盡力了。

I've done everything I could.

▶我搞砸了。

I messed up.

▶這不是我該做的。

This is not my job.

▶不要浪費時間。

Don't waste time.

▶這令人無法接受！

This is not acceptable!

▶這水準不夠。

This is not up to par.

This is not up to standard.

▶你應該可以做的更好！

You should have done better!

You can do better.

▶你要學的東西還很多！

You still have a lot to learn!

▶我們人手不足。

We are short of hands.

▶我需要多一點時間。

I need more time.

Give me more time.

▶遭透了！

This sucks!

Sucks!

快樂

▶她對他微笑了一下。

She gives him a smile.

▶我們笑到眼淚都流出來了。

We laugh till tears come.

└註：laugh 泛指笑聲。

▶我不喜歡她的假笑。

I don't like her smirk.

└註：smirk 是有一點自鳴得意或輕視的笑。

▶有些人在掩嘴偷笑。

Some people snickered.
Some people sniggered.

▶他們在偷偷笑我。

They snickered at me.

└註：通常是沒有發出聲音，私下偷偷的取笑，不是很尊重的表情。

▶他們看著照片咯咯地笑著。

They are chuckling over the pictures.

└註：沒有發出聲音地笑或笑得很小聲，自己偷偷的笑，心情是滿足喜悅的。

▶那個笑話惹得她咯咯嬌笑。

The joke makes her giggle.

└註：giggle 形容短而急促的笑聲。多指小孩或女孩子們發出的笑聲。

▶女生們吃吃的笑著。

The girls titter.

└註：跟 giggle 差不多，形容短而急促的笑聲。或因緊張、發窘時產生的笑聲。

▶(那位電影明星一現身，)小姐們便開始嘻笑。

The ladies cackle (when the movie star showes up).

└註：多形容女子或小孩嘰嘰喳喳地笑語聲。也可用來形容尖銳粗厲的聲音。

▶他露齒一笑表示贊同。

He grins his approval.

└註：微笑角度較大，露出牙齒的笑容。

▶那壞人突然狂笑。

The bad guy guffaws.

└註：突然地粗聲大笑。

▶他對我的建議嗤之以鼻。

He sneers at my suggestion.

▶我可以興災樂禍。

I could gloat over this.

▶她的眼神看起來很快樂。

I can feel the joy in her eyes.

▶我今天看起來神采飛揚。

I am bright and shining today.

生氣

▶他的臉因為盛怒而漲得通紅。

His face turns red with rage.

▶他的聲音使我很煩躁。

His voice irritates me.

▶他挑起戰爭。

He provokes the war.

▶他激怒那隻狗。

He provoks the dog.

▶你很煩呢。

You are so annoying.

▶你很令我生氣。

You make me mad.

You make me angry.

▶不要生氣/不要被激怒。

Don't get mad.

VOCABULARY
相關單字

outrageous	勃然大怒的
furious	狂怒的
quarrelsome	愛爭吵的

悲傷

▶她哭的更傷心了。

She cried even harder.

▶他整夜呻吟。

He moaned all night.

▶那位母親哀泣著。

The mother weeps.

▶她在夜晚悲苦地哭泣著。

She weeps bitterly in the night.

▶那位父親深深的嘆了一口氣。

The father sighed deeply.

▶他哀悼了許多天。

He mourned for many days.

▶她在啜泣。

She sobs.

▶她痛苦地呻吟著。

She groans in pain.

▶我們哀悼著深深的悲痛。

We mourn with deep grief.

好/惡

▶我喜歡跟你在一起。

I enjoy being with you.

▶我喜歡你。

I like you.

▶我在乎你。

I care for you.

▶我欽佩你。/我欣賞你。/我羨慕你。

I admire you.

▶我妒忌你。

I envy you.
I am jealous of you.

▶她吃醋了。

She is jealousy.

▶我暗戀你。/我愛慕你。

I fancy you.
I have a crush on you.

▶他們倆來電。

They are clicking.
They have chemistry.

└ 註：chemistry 也可以做「默契」的意思。

▶我好想回家。

I desire to go home.

▶我珍愛我的小孩。

I cherish my child.

└ 註：cherish 更強調愛護，保護，溫柔照顧的愛。

▶我寧願回家。

I prefer to go home.

└ 註：prefer 出現時，表示同時有兩種以上的選擇，prefer 之後接的是說
　　話者「比較想」做的事。

▶她是我最喜歡的。

She is my favorite.

└ 註：favorite 表示多樣選擇中「最喜歡」的東西。

▶我不可自拔地愛你。

I am addicted to you.

▶我恨那個(事件，物品)。

I hate that.

▶你真丟臉。

Shame on you.

▶這真是尷尬。

This is awkward.

▶我好尷尬(窘)。

I am embarrassed.

不安

▶我覺得不自在。

I feel uneasy.
I feel uncomfortable.

▶他不安地玩弄他的戒指。

He fidgets with his ring.

▶我有一點焦躁不安。

I am a little bit restless.
I am anxious.

害怕/失望

▶不要驚慌。

Don't panic.

▶我很怕那條狗。

I am afraid of that dog.

▶我被嚇到了。

I am frightened.
I am scared.

▶那個小孩被嚇壞了。

The kid is terrified.

▶我嚇壞了。

I was horrified.

▶恐怖！

Spooky!

└ 註：形容鬼影幢幢的感覺。

▶恐怖！

Creepy!

└ 註：形容毛骨悚然，不含而慄的感覺。

▶嚇死我了。

I am so shocked.
What a shock!
This is a shock.

└ 註：shock 不一定有恐怖的感覺，驚愕、驚訝、出乎意料時都可以用
shock。

▶這真可怕。

This is horrible.
This is dreadful.

▶我感到失望。

I feel disappointed.
I am disappointed.

▶我們感到沮喪。

We are frustrated.
We are depressed.

驚訝

▶你真令人驚訝。/你太棒了。

You are amazing.

▶我真驚訝。

I am so surprised.

▶你真令人出乎意料。

You are full of surprise.

▶我們對她的聲音驚為天人。

We are astonished by her voice.

平靜

▶請保持安靜。

Keep quiet.

▶不要動喔。

Hold still.

▶願她平靜長眠。

May she rest in peace.

└註：在葬禮等場合的常用語。

▶冷靜下來！

Calm down!
Cool down!

擔憂/心情煩躁/心裡不舒服

▶別擔心。

Don't worry.

▶我沒什麼可擔心的。

Nothing worries me.

▶我很擔心你。

I am worried about you.

▶我心裡有些事情在煩惱。

I am troubled.
Something is bothering me.

▶我心情不好。

I am low.
I am down-hearted.

▶我沒有心情。

I am not in the mood.

▶請勿打擾。

Don't disturb.

▶那噪音打擾(妨礙)到我了。

That noise disturbs me.
That noise is troubling me.

▶抱歉打擾了。

Sorry to disturb you.

▶不用你費心。

Don't bother.

▶何必多事？

Why bother?

▶那個壞消息令我很難過。

The bad news upset me.

▶我對我的生活感到失望。

I am upset about my life.

▶我渴望去那裡

I am anxious to go there.

無聊

▶我覺得無聊。

I am bored.

▶這是一個無聊的故事。

This is a boring story.

▶這個故事很呆板乏味。

This story is dull.

▶那真是冗長而乏味。

It's so tedious.

It's so boring.

└ 註：形容長篇大論的演講或任何時間拉得很長的表演令人覺得無聊。

冷酷

▶這個地方充滿敵意。

This place is hostile.

▶她看起不太友善。

She looks unfriendly.

└ 註：相反詞就是 friendly。

▶你真是鐵石心腸。

You are so cold.

You are so cold hearted.

思考

▶我要想一下。

I need to think about that.

▶我要考慮下一步。

I am considering my next step.

▶他考慮了一下。

He pondered.

▶我在打坐(冥想)。

I am meditating.

猜想/假設/想像/不確定/猶豫

▶猜猜看吧。

Make a guess.

▶我就知道！/早知道是這樣！/我早猜到了！

I figured.

└註：事情的發展不出所料。

▶我相信是這樣！/我想應該是這樣！

I believe (so)!

▶我想是吧！/大概是吧！

I suppose (so)!

I guess (so)!

└註：事情還沒發生，說話者猜想事情的發展。

▶假設這是正確的…

Assume this is correct...

Suppose this is correct...

└註：事情還沒發生，但說話者預設事情的發展如果是正確的條件下，
結果將會是如何如何。

▶我無法想像。

I can't imagine.

▶我很懷疑(那有可能嗎)。

I doubt it.

└註：對談論的話題表示懷疑及不確定感。

▶我懷疑她的誠信問題。

I suspect her honesty.

└註：對談論的話題表示懷疑及不信任。

▶我不確定她愛不愛他。

I wonder if she loves him.

▶我還不確定。

I am still not sure.

I am still uncertain.

▶我對那件事很好奇。

I am curious about that.

└註：curious 有「想知道更多，窺探」的意思。

▶你在混淆我。

You are confusing me.

└註：因多項原因而感到混淆，迷惑。

▶我弄混了。/我搞不清楚了。

I am confused

I am mixed up.

▶不要遲疑。

Don't hesitate.

└註：鼓勵用語。

吵架/口角/爭吵

▶滾！

Get lost!
Get out!

▶停止！/不要再説了！/不要再吵了！

Stop!
Knock it out!
Quit fighting.

▶我真的很失望！

I am very disappointed.

▶饒了我吧！

Give me a break.

▶真是鬼話連篇！

This is nonsense!

▶我受不了了！

I can't take it anymore!

▶你瘋了嗎？

Are you insane?
Are you crazy?
Are you out of your mind?

▶那不是我的錯！

It's not my fault!

▶不要當個討厭鬼！

Don't be a pain in the ass.
Don't be a pain in my neck.

▶別那樣和我說話！

Don't talk to me like that!

▶你快把我氣死了。

You piss me off!
You make me so mad.
You make me so angry.

▶你是怎麼回事？

What's wrong with you?

▶你自找的!

You asked for it!

▶你敢！

How dare you!

▶胡說！

Bull shit!

▶不要廢話！

Shut up!
Cut the crap.

▶我受夠了！

I am fed up!

▶簡直是瘋了！
　真是蠢透了！

This is insane!
This is nuts!

▶你在恐嚇我嗎？

Are you threatening me?

▶這真是無禮。

This is rude.

▶這簡直就是侮辱。

This is an insult.

▶我們吵了一架。

We had a fight.
We had a quarrel.
We had an argument.

▶我們吵了一架。

We had some disagreement.

└ 註：跟 fight 比起來較優雅的說法。

▶我必須捍衛我的權利。

I have to fight over my right.

▶我們經常為了它吵架。

We often quarrel about it.
We often fight about it.
We often argue about it.

疲倦

▶我累了。

I am tired.

▶我累壞了。

I am tired out.
I am beat.

▶我已經精疲力竭了。

I am pooped.
I am drained.
I am exhausted.
I am burned out.
I've run out of steam.

▶我累昏了。

I am trashed.
I am totally knocked out.

└註：喝醉了，醉到昏死過去也可以用這個說法。

▶我喝醉了。

I got wasted.

▶我累了一天。

It's been a long day.

└註：人在覺得疲憊時，常覺得時間過得很慢，所以用「過了很長的一天」來表達自己很累。

Chapter 6

聊天-食衣住

談話中最基本的生活面

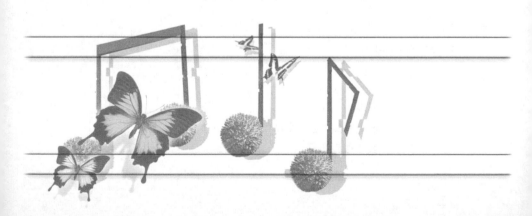

食物的味道

▶嚐起來如何？

How is it?
How does it taste?
What's it like?

▶好酸。

Sour.
Acid.
Vinegary.
This is tart.

▶ 好甜。

Sweet.
Sugary.

▶好鹹。

Salty.

▶好辣。

Hot
Spicy.

▶好苦。

Bitter.
Dry.

▶大蒜味

Garlicky flavor.

▶真有嚼勁！

Chewy.

▶太韌了。

肉太硬了。

Tough.

▶真酥脆！

Crispy.

▶真鬆脆！

Crunchy!

▶真鬆軟！

Soft!

▶真濃郁！

This is so rich.

▶真滑順！

Smooth!

▶真多汁！

Juicy!

▶真新鮮！

Very fresh!

▶美味極了！

　　Yummy!
　　Tasty!
　　Delicious!

▶味道還不錯。

　　Nice.
　　It's good.

▶好噁心！

　　Disgusting!
　　Yuck!
　　Gross!

▶太油了。

　　This is too oily.
　　Greasy.

▶味道好奇怪。

　　It tastes funny.
　　It tastes weird.
　　It tastes strange.

▶沒什麼味道。

　　This is tasteless.
　　Unsavory.
　　Weak.

食物的烹調

▶這(食物)煮得很透。

This is all cooked.
It is perfectly cooked.

▶(食物)煮成金黃色。

Cook till it is brown.

└註：brown 所指的是表皮微焦的狀態。常用在表示麵包烤得微焦，或是食物炸/煎成金黃色的樣子。

▶這(食物)沒有熟吧。

This is not done.
This is underdone.
This is raw.

▶這(食物)太熟了吧。

This is over done.
This is too hard.

└註：口感軟嫩的食物，比如蛋、肉、海鮮類，如果煮過頭會變得太硬，就是 hard。

▶這(食物)焦掉了。

This is burnt.
This is too dark.

└註：麵包烤得太焦用 dark 這個字。

▶這(食物)不夠焦。

This is too light.

食物不能吃了

►(食物)不新鮮。

This is not fresh.

►這壞掉了吧。

The food has gone bad.
This has gone bad.
This is spoiled.
This is ruined.

└ 註：一般食物壞掉都可以用上述的說法。

►蛋糕不新鮮。

This cake has gone stale.

└ 註：stale是食物變硬、變乾、不新鮮的意思。用在形容蛋糕，麵包等
　　食物。

►(食物)受潮了。

This has become damp.
This is soggy.

└ 註：常用在形容麵包或餅乾。

►肉類蔬果腐敗。

This is rotten.

└ 註：rotten是腐敗的意思。用在形容蔬果肉類食物。

►形容食物酸掉了。

This milk has gone sour.

└ 註：酸掉了的意思。用在形容牛奶，乳酪等會發酵的食品。

▶奶油臭掉了。

The butter is rancid.

└ 註：rancid 指油類製品過期的臭油味。

▶壞掉的(食物)。

Bad food.

└ 註：bad 可以形容所有腐壞的食物。因此，要表達食物壞掉了，只要在食物名稱前面加 bad，就可以囉。

▶啤酒/可樂沒氣了。

The beer is flat./The coke is flat.

└ 註：車子的輪胎沒氣了也是 flat。例如：flat tire.

外食或自行下廚

▶叫外送吧！

Let's order some delivery.
Let's order XX!

└ 註：將 XX 代換為 Pizza (比薩) 或任何有外送服務的食物即可。

▶上館子吃飯吧！

Let's eat out!
Let's grab a bite.
Let's go to XX.(餐廳名)

└ 註：直接說餐廳名也可以喔。

▶我自己準備午餐。

I prepare my own lunch.

▶今天自己煮飯吧。

Let's cook.

▶可以吃晚餐囉！

Dinner is served
Dinner is ready.
Supper is served.

▶請幫忙把碗筷擺好。

Set the table, please?

▶桌子準備好了。

Table is ready.
Table is set.

訂位

▶我要訂位。

I want to book a table.
I would like to make a reservation.

▶我沒有訂位。

I don't have a reservation.

▶我們有五個人(用餐)。

Party of 5!
Table for 5!

▶只有我一個人(用餐)。

Just me.
Just one.

▶我們（餐廳）都訂滿了。

> We are all booked.
> We are booked up.
> We're full today.

▶我們（餐廳）已經超訂了。

> We are overbooked.

▶我們還有空桌/空位。

> We still have a table available.

▶你們還有空位嗎？

> Do you have table for us?

▶請問還有靠窗的桌子嗎？

> Is there a table available by the window?

▶幾點供應餐。

> When is the meal served?
> When is the restaurant open?

▶我們（餐廳）可以訂位。
我們接受訂位。

> We are availabe for booking.

準備點餐

▶請給我菜單。

　　Menu, please.
　　Can I have a menu?

▶可以點菜了嗎？

　　Ready to order?

▶我要點菜。

　　Order, please.

▶我們可以點菜了。

　　We are ready.

▶等一下再點。

　　Wait.
　　Wait a moment.

▶你們有什麼？

　　Do you have any suggestions?
　　What do you have?

▶我可以幫你們點菜嗎？

　　May I take your order, please?

▶要點餐了嗎？

　　Ready?

點餐

▶你們的招牌菜是什麼？

　　What's your special?

▶請給我今日特餐。

　　Today's special.

▶請給我主廚特餐。

　　Chef's special, please.

▶請給我一份雞肉。

　　A chicken, please.

　　Give me a chicken.

　└註：點菜最簡單的方式就是直接說出菜名，或乾脆指菜單給服務人員
　　　　看就好囉！

▶一號餐。

　　Number one.

　　Combo number one.

　└註：在速食店裡面點套餐時用。

▶我也要同樣的餐點。

　　Same, please.

　　I'd like the same.

　　Make it two.

　└註：如果想要點跟朋友一樣的東西，在朋友點完餐跟服務生說 "Make
　　　　it two"。

牛排的煮法

▶牛排要幾分熟呢？

How would you like it?

How would you like your steak?

How would you like to cook it?

How would you like to cook your steak?

▶全熟。

熟透了。

Well done.

All cooked.

All done.

▶七（八）分熟。

Medium Well.

▶五分熟。

Medium.

▶三分熟的。

Medium Rare.

▶生的。

Rare.

蛋的煮法

▶你希望怎麼烹調雞蛋？

How would you like your eggs?

▶請給我一個煎蛋捲。

An omelet, please.

▶荷包蛋。

Fried egg.

▶單煎一面的荷包蛋。

Sunny-side up

▶兩面煎(不要太老，蛋黃是生的)。

Over easy, please.

▶兩面煎 (蛋黃全熟)。

Over hard.

▶蒸蛋。

Poached egg.

▶炒蛋。

Scrambled egg.

▶半熟的水煮蛋。

Soft-boiled egg.

▶全熟的水煮蛋。

Hard-boiled egg.

在餐廳常點的飲料

▶需要飲料嗎？

Any drink?/Beverage?/Care for some drink?

▶請給我可樂/冰茶。

Coke/Ice tea, please.

▶檸檬水。

Lemonade.

▶給我水就好了。

Just water.

在咖啡廳點飲料

▶大杯/中杯/小杯

Grande/Tall/Short

▶低咖啡因

Decaf

▶低脂/無脂

Low fat/Non-fat

▶奶精和糖

Milk and sugar.

續杯怎麼說

▶我可以續杯嗎？

　　Could I get a refill?

▶續杯多少錢？

　　How much are refills?

其他軟性飲料

▶軟性飲料。

　　Soft drink.

　　└ 註：不含酒精的飲料。

▶拿鐵

　　Latte

▶義式濃縮

　　Espresso

▶摩卡咖啡

　　Cafe Mocha

▶咖啡歐雷

　　Cafe au lait.

▶黑咖啡

Black Coffee.

└ 註：不加糖及奶精的咖啡

▶茉莉花茶

Jasmine tea.

▶伯爵茶

Earl grey tea.

在酒吧點飲料

▶我請你喝飲料。

Have a drink on me.
Let me buy you a drink.

▶給我啤酒。

Beer, please.

▶生啤酒

Draft beer.

▶黑啤酒

Stout beer.

▶威士忌加冰。

Scotch on the rocks.

▶香檳

　　Champagne.

▶酒吧老闆請喝啤酒！

　　Beer on the house!

▶我請客！

　　This is my treat!

　　This is on me!

▶想喝點什麼嗎？

　　Can I fix you a drink?

調味料

▶有鹽嗎？

　　Salt, please.

▶請給我番茄醬。

　　Ketchup, please.

▶需要醋嗎？

　　Vinegar?

▶有糖嗎？

　　Sugar?

　　└ 註：簡單的問句，由服務人員口中說出來，意思是「需要 xx 嗎？」
　　　　如果由顧客口中說出，意思則是「有沒有 xx？」

▶加點糖也可以。

It could do with a little sugar.

▶請把鹽遞過來，好嗎？

Pass the salt, please.

▶芥茉醬

Mustard.

▶胡椒。

Pepper.

▶沾醬。

Dressing.

要求其他服務

▶給我一根吸管

Give me a straw.

▶再來一份。

One more.

└ 註：跟前面所提到的 make it two 不同。One more 是追加一份的意思。

▶請給我多一點醬料。

More dressing, please.

More sauce, please.

└ 註：dressing 多指沙拉醬料。Sauce 指餐點的醬汁。

▶請再給我一支叉子。

Please give me another fork.

▶幫我打包。

Doggy bag this.

▶請給我紙巾,好嗎?

Can I have a napkin, please?

▶請排隊等候。

Please wait in the line.

特殊飲食習慣

▶我在節食。

I am on a diet.

└註:diet 指減肥餐或營養餐。只要是醫生規定的用餐計畫,比如說忌食某些食物,某些營養應多攝取…等,都算是 diet。

▶我在吃營養餐。

I am on a special meal plan.

▶我是素食者。

I am a vegetarian.

▶不要加辣。

No spice.

▶非吸煙區

No smoking.

No smoking area.

Non-smoking section.

▶吸煙區

Smoking.

Smoking area.

Smoking section.

▶窗邊的桌子

A table with a view.

A table by the window.

內用/外帶

▶外帶。

Out.

To go.

Take away.

Take out.

▶內用。

In.

For here.

Eat here.

Dine here.

Dine in.

結帳

▶付現或刷卡?

Cash or credit card?

▶買單！

Check, Please!

▶我請客。

這次算我的。

My treat.

It's on me.

I'll get the check.

▶該你請客囉！

你請客啦！(開玩笑式地)

It's your turn!

This is on you!

You get the bill!

▶一起算就好了。

Just one check.

▶各付各的。

Go Dutch!?

Separate checks.

▶您的收據。

Your receipt, sir.

其它

▶我們謹候您的光臨。

We will be expecting you.

▶謝謝您的光臨。

Thank you for coming.

▶給小費。

Tip.
Give a tip.

▶我吃完了。

I'm finished.
I'm through.

▶吃完了嗎？

Finished?
Are you through?

▶我們吃完了。(可以結帳離開了)

We are through.

▶你剛剛有給女侍者小費嗎？

Did you tip the waitress?

└ 註：男侍者是 waiter。

▶歡迎！

Welcome!

衣 洗衣服

▶我要去洗衣服。

I need to do my laundry.

I am doing my laundry

└ 註：中文說「洗」衣服的動詞「洗」，在英文裡用 do 表示，簡單吧！

▶有沒有要洗的衣服？

Do you have any laundry?

Have you got any laundry?

▶我有些髒衣服要洗。

I have some dirty laundry.

▶我洗了兩大桶衣服。

I did two loads of laundry.

▶要加洗衣精。

Add soap.

Put soap.

▶要加柔軟精。

Add fabric softener.

▶加漂白劑。

Add bleach.

▶漂白襯衫。

Bleach the shirt.

└ 註：bleach 可以直接做動詞使用。

▶(深淺色)分開洗。

Wash separately.

Wash dark and light color separately.

▶我的衣服被染到其他顏色了。

The color bled onto my dress.

The dress had color bled on it.

└ 註：bled 的原型動詞是 bleed。

▶哪裡可以晾衣服？

Where can I hang my laundry?

▶把乾的衣服收進來。

Collect the dry laundry.

Bring in the laundry.

Grab your clothes from the line.

└ 註：line 指的是曬衣繩。

▶衣服不夠乾。

This is not dry enough.

▶我必須要折衣服。

I need to fold my clothes.

送洗衣服

▶把衣服送洗吧。

Send it to the laundry.
Take it to the cleaner.
I'd like to have it laundered.

▶這必須手洗。

This should be washed by hand.

▶用洗衣機洗就好了。

Just machine wash.

▶水洗就好了。

Just wash it.

▶這件要乾洗。

Dry clean this.
This needs to be dry-cleaned.

▶這不能乾洗。

Don't dry clean it.

▶這污漬很難洗。

The stain is stubborn.

▶請把污漬去除。

Make the stain go away.
Please remove the stain.

▶這污漬恐怕洗不到掉。

The stain won't go.
The stain won't come out.
The stain won't wash out.
The stain won't be removed.

▶不要漿衣服。

No starch, please.

▶什麼時候洗好?

When will it be ready.

▶這件衣服我今晚就要。

I need it tonight.

▶去洗衣店拿衣服。

Pick up laundry.
Collect laundry.
Get the laundry back.

▶我忘記去拿衣服了。

I forgot to collect my laundry.

▶這不是我的衣服。

This is not mine.

▶有一件遺失了。

There is one piece missing.

▶衣服洗壞了。

This is damaged.

▶衣服縮水了。

> It is shrunk.
>
> └ 註：shrunk 的原型動詞是 shrink。

▶衣服褪色了。

> It's discolored.
> The color faded.
> The color is washed off.
> The color came out.

▶我的白襯衫都被染紅了。

> My white shirts are all pink now.

▶衣服皺皺的。

> It is wrinkled.
> It is full of creases.

▶我的襯衫毀了。

> My shirts are ruined.

▶這是我的洗衣單。

> Here is my laundry slip.

▶請幫我燙襯衫。

> Please press these shirts for me.

▶你可以幫我把衣服掛起來嗎？

> Can you hang this up for me?

自助洗衣

▶這是乾衣機。

This is a dryer.

▶這是投幣式洗衣機。

This is coin-operated washer.

▶投幣(進洗衣機)。

Insert coins.

Put coins in the machine.

▶我的硬幣卡住了

It is jammed.

My coin is stuck.

It gets stuck in the slot.

▶蓋上洗衣機的蓋子。

Close the lid.

▶在洗衣服了。

It's washing.

▶在沖滌了。

It's rinsing。

▶在脫水了。

It's spinning.

衣服的質料

▶這是什麼料子做的？

What is this made of?

▶這是不會褪色的。

This is colorfast.

▶是絲質的。

It's silk.

VOCABULARY
相關單字

linen	麻	yarn	紗
lycra	萊卡	satin	緞
velvet	絲絨	flannel	法蘭絨
leather	皮	wool	羊毛
cashmere	喀什米爾羊毛	nylon	尼龍
blends	混紡	cotton	棉
Egyptian cotton	埃及棉		
denim	丹寧布，牛仔布		

衣服的功能

▶這是防水的。

This is water proof.

This is water resistant.

▶這可以擋雨。

This is shower proof.

└註：下毛毛雨時可以當作雨衣使用，尤其常見於風衣式的外套上。

▶這是防風的。

This is wind proof.

This is wind resistant.

▶這是透氣的。

This is breathable.

This is moisture permeable.

▶這有抗菌的功能。

This is anti-bacterial.

▶這是防臭布料。

This is odor preventing fabric.

▶這有排汗速乾的功能。

This is fast dry.

▶這會防靜電。

This is anti-static.

訂做衣服

▶這是訂做的。

This is tailor-made.

This is custom-made.

This is customized.

This is custom-fit.

This is made-to-measure.

This is made-to-order.

▶我來為你量身。

Can I take your measurements?

▶請幫我量身。

Please measure me.

▶他是一位裁縫師。

He is a tailor.

└註：裁製男裝的裁縫師。

He is a dressmaker.

└註：裁製女裝的裁縫師。

He is a couturier.

└註：裁製高級訂製服的裁縫師。

▶(女性的)三圍數字

Measurements.

Vital statistics.

▶我為你量頸圍。

Let me take your neck size.

▶胸圍

Chest measurement.

└ 註：泛指男人或女人的胸圍。

Breasts measurement.

Bust measurement.

└ 註：breasts 和 bust 指女人的胸圍。

▶腰圍/臀圍

Waist measurement./Hip measurement.

▶我來試穿。

I come for suit fitting.

└ 註：裁縫師做好衣服後，客人在取走前做最後的試穿動作。

購買成衣

▶這是我最喜歡的品牌。

This is my favorite brand.

▶我可以試穿嗎？

Can I try it on?

I want to try it on.

└ 註：買成衣時試穿。

▶你穿幾號？

What's your size?

What size are you?

What size do you wear?

What size do you take?

▶我穿四號。

Size four.
I am a size four.

▶這件有沒有我的尺寸？

Do you have this in my size?

▶這件是你的尺寸。

This is your size.

▶沒有你的尺寸。

We don't have your size.

▶有小一點的嗎？

Do you have a smaller size?

▶有大一點的嗎？

Do you have larger size?

▶他喜歡寬鬆一點的衣服。

He prefers baggy clothes.
He likes loose-fitting clothes.

▶我喜歡合身的衣服。

I like the fitted look.

▶那看起來很邋遢。

It looks sloppy.

└註：衣服過大，看起來鬆散不合身。

試穿衣服

▶試衣間在哪裡？

Where is the fitting room?
Where is the dressing room?

▶合身嗎？

How does it fit?

▶你喜歡這個寬鬆度嗎？

Do you like the fit?

▶衣服不合身。

It doesn't fit.
It looks ill-fitting.

▶衣服很合身。

It fits well.
It fits perfectly.
This is just my size.
Very comfortable fit.

▶這很適合你。

It fits you.
It fits you well.
It looks great on you.
Very nice fit.
Very good fit.

▶這跟棕色很配。

    It goes perfectly with brown.

▶我穿著太大。

    It's too big for me

▶我穿著太小。

    It's too small for me.

▶這裡有點緊。

    It's a little tight here.

▶這很貼身。

    This is tight fitting./This is skin-tight.

▶這裡有點鬆。

    It's a little loose here.

▶這裡放鬆一點。

    Make it a little loose here.

▶太長了。

    It's too long.

▶太短了。

    It's too short.

修改/縫補衣服

▶請幫我修改衣服。

Please alter this.
Please adjust it.
Please tailor my dress.

▶我想修改一下衣服。

I need to make some alterations.

▶你們有修改服務嗎？

Do you do alterations?
Could I have this hemmed?

▶請幫我縫補衣服

Please mend my dress.

▶釦子掉了。

The button is missing.

▶拉鍊卡住了/壞了。

The zipper is broken.
The zip got stuck.

▶縫線掉了。

The threads come unraveled.

▶縫線沒縫好。

The thread is undone.

穿衣服/使用飾品

▶衣服穿好。

Get dressed.

▶把扣子扣好。

Button your shirt.
Button the button.

└ 註：第一個 button 是動詞，第二個 button 是名詞。

▶拉上拉鍊。

Zip up (the zipper).
Tug on your zip.
Zip (your dress) up.

▶把袖子捲起來。

Roll up your sleeves.

▶把袖子放下來。

Unroll your sleeves.

▶把襯衫紮進去。

Tuck in your shirt.

▶把外套的帽子拉上。

Pull on your parka.
Put on your hood.

▶衣服穿好。/把身體包好(沐浴後)。/把身體蓋起來(用棉被)。

Cover yourself up.

▶穿上外套吧！

Put on your coat.
Put on your jacket.

└ 註：put on 就是穿上或戴上的意思，幾乎所有的衣飾都可以使用這個動詞。

▶脫掉你的外套。

Take off your coat.

└ 註：take off 就是脫掉或拿下的意思，幾乎所有的衣飾都可以使用這個動詞。

▶他匆匆脫掉衣服。

He slipped off his clothes.

▶打個蝴蝶結。

Make a bow.

▶把鞋帶繫緊。

Fasten your shoelace.

▶我有擦香水。

I wear perfume.
I apply perfume.

▶我有戴項鍊。

I wear a necklace.

└ 註：戴項鍊用 wear。

衣服的樣式

▶你今天穿什麼？

What do you wear today?

▶這是 V 領的式樣。

It's a V neck.

▶這是高領的。

It's a turtle neck.

▶我上班要穿制服。

I wear uniform at work.

▶我穿 T 恤。

I wear a T-shirt.

▶我今天穿短袖。

I wear short sleeves today.

▶我總是穿牛仔褲。

I use to wear jeans.

▶我穿了一條新褲子。

I wear a new pair of pants.

└ 註：褲子有兩條褲管，所以字尾要加上表示複數的 s 喔。

▶我穿了一雙鞋

I am wearing a pair of shoes.

└ 註：鞋子也有兩隻，所以字尾也要加上表示複數的 s。

評論穿著

▶穿的很帥/漂亮喔！

Nice outfit!

▶你今天穿的很瀟灑喔！

You look smart today.

▶你看起來真時髦。

Your look so chic.

▶很隨興喔。

Very casual!

▶你穿得很性感喔！

You look sexy.

▶這是一件很可愛的背心。

This is a cute vest.

▶穿起來很舒服的感覺。

It feels comfortable.

▶你今天看起來很酷喔！

You look cool today.

▶這是最前衛流行的設計。

It's a trendy design.

▶剪裁不錯喔。

Nice cut.

整理衣物

▶折衣服。

Fold cloth.

▶不要弄皺衣服。

Don't crease it.

Don't crumple it.

▶那樣衣服會變皺。

It will wrinkle.

▶把(衣服)放到衣櫥裡。

Put it in the closet.

Hang it in the wardrobe.

▶請幫我燙平衣服。

Please have it pressed.

That needs to be pressed.

Please iron my dress.

Please do the ironing.

Please iron out the wrinkles.

▶把你的鞋子放在這裡。

Put your shoes here.

▶把帽子掛在鉤子上。

Hang your hat on the hook.

▶整理衣櫃。

Organize your wardrobe.

▶整理我冬季的衣服。

Organize my winter wardrobe.

└註：wardrobe 也引申代表你所有的服裝。

▶衣櫃裡塞不下了。

There is no space in my wardrobe.

▶衣櫥還有很多空間。

We still have plenty space in the closet.

▶把我的外套掛進衣櫥。

Hang my coat in the closet.

▶把這個放到抽屜裡。

Put this in the drawer.

▶掛在衣帽架上。

Put on the coat rack.
Hang on the coat rack.

└註：hat rack 就是帽架。

▶用衣夾夾住。

Clip it with a clothespin.

▶用衣架掛起來。

Hang with a hanger.

尺寸的標示

▶大號，或以 L 表示

Large size (L)

▶中號，或以 M 表示

Medium size (M)

▶小號，或以 S 表示

Small size (S)

▶特大號，或以 XL 表示

Extra large (XL)

▶特小號，或以 XS 表示

Extra small (XS)

▶加大尺碼的衣服

Plus size clothing

▶超小尺寸服裝

Petite clothing

└註：clothing 是衣服的總稱。

▶適合任何尺寸

Free size

One size

跟誰住

▶你和誰同住？

Who do you live with?
Who are you rooming with?

▶我跟朋友一起住。

I live with a friend.

▶我跟家人一起住。

I live with my family.

▶我自己住。

I live alone.

▶我和朋友合住一間屋子。

I share a house with a friend.

▶我們可以一起合租一層公寓。

We can rent an apartment together.

▶我們同住一間房間。

We share a room.

▶沒有隱私。

There is no privacy.

▶我住宿舍

I live in a dorm.
I live in an accommodation.

租房子

▶我租了一間公寓。

I rent an apartment.

▶這是出租嗎?

Is this for rent?

▶這是賣屋嗎?

Is this for sale?

▶我要找房子租。

I am looking for a house for rent.

▶我將這間房間轉/分租給 XX。

I sublet the room to XX.

▶出租。

For rent.
To let.
To lease.
For lease.

▶這(房子)是租的。

This is rental.

▶房租多少錢？

What is the rate?
What is the rental price?

▶我可以到處看看嗎？

Can I take a look?

▶我們可以看一下廚房嗎？

Can we see the kitchen?

▶房間有傢俱嗎？

Is it furnished?

▶傢俱是新的嗎？

Is the furniture new?

▶大約每週美金30元。

It costs US$30 per week.

▶可以養貓嗎？

Are cats allowed?

▶我要這間公寓。

I will take this apartment.

▶請預付US$300元作為押金。

Please make US$300 deposit.

▶請預付一個月租金。

Please pay a one month rent in advance.

▶我什麼時候可以搬進來？

When can I move in?

住旅館

▶我住在一家旅館裡。

I stay in a hotel.

▶我打電話來訂房間。

Can I book a room?

Can I make a reservation?

▶我需要一個單人房。

I'd like a single room.

▶一間單人房。

A single bedroom.

▶一間有兩張單人床的房間。

A twin bedroom.

▶有一張雙人床的房間。

A double bedroom.

▶有衛浴設備的房間，也就是套房。

A suite.

▶我要住兩晚。

I will stay for 2 nights.

▶我已經預約了一間房間。

I have reserved a room

▶以 XX(姓名)訂房。

It's under XX.
The reservation is under XX.

▶(這間房間)要價多少錢？

What is the price?
What are the rates?

▶您會住多久？

How long will you stay?

▶我何時可以住進來？

What time can I check in?

▶服務費包括在房款內嗎？

Is the service charge included?
Does this include service charge?

▶請給我非吸煙樓層。

Please give me a non-smoking floor.

▶請給我安靜一點的房間。

I need a quiet room.

▶請給我有景觀的房間

I need a room a with view.

▶請給我低樓層的房間。

I need a room on the lower floor.

▶請給我高樓層的房間。

I need a higher floor room.

▶你們有沒有床大一點的房間？

Do you have a room with larger bed?

▶我要 king size 的床。

I need a king size bed.

▶我要 queen size 的床。

I need a queen size bed.

▶我要加床。

I need an extra bed.

▶King size 的房間價格較高。

King size bedroom costs more.

▶有沒有便宜些的房間？

Cheaper?
Do you have a cheaper room?

▶請幫我搬行李。

Please carry my suitcase.

▶退房的時間是幾點鐘？

When is the check out time?

▶旅館進住。

Check in, please.

▶旅館退房。

Check out, please.

▶我要退房了。

I'm checking out.

▶喚醒服務。

Morning call service.
Wake up call service.

▶有給我的留言嗎？

Any message for me?
Any message for room XXX?(房號)

▶你能推薦另一個旅館嗎？

Could you recommend another hotel?

└ 註：萬一旅館客滿時，請服務人員建議另一家旅館。

▶這要放進旅館的保險櫃。

I need to put this in the hotel safe.

▶我可不可以先把行李留在櫃檯？

Can I leave my baggage at the front desk?

▶客房服務。

Room service.

▶請將晚餐送到我房間。

Please send dinner to my room.

▶請送盥洗用具上來給我。

Please send a bathroom kit to my room.

▶請多送一條毯子。

I need an extra blanket.
Please send me one more blanket.

▶請多送一個枕頭。

I need an extra pillow.
Please send one more pillow.

▶床單上有髒污。

There is a stain on my sheet.

▶(旅館)酒吧在哪裡？

Where is the bar?

▶預約 SPA.

I need to make an appointment for the SPA.

▶我能使用健身房嗎？

Can I use the gym?

▶我們在大廳見吧。

Let's meet in the lobby.

房內隔局

▶我們有兩房一廳。

We have 2 rooms and one living room.

▶我住在一個有房間和廚房的公寓裡。

I live in a flat with bedrooms and kitchen.

▶我們共用廚房。

We share a kitchen.

▶我們共用浴室。

We share a bathroom.

住屋環境

▶附近地區。

The neighborhood.

▶附近有網咖。

There are Internet cafes.

▶附近有洗衣店嗎？

Is there a laundry nearby?

▶有沒有提款機？

Are there ATMs?

▶去那裏要花多久時間？

How long will it take?

▶有去 XX 的巴士嗎？

Is there a bus to XX?

▶環境會不會很吵？

Is it noisy?

▶離 XX 遠嗎？

Is it far from XX?

▶離 XX 不遠。

Close to XX.
Not far from XX.
Near the XX.

▶不遠，只有幾步路。

Just a walk away.
Near by....
Close by....

▶五分鐘車程。

Five minutes by car.
Five minutes drive.
Five minutes drive away.

▶五分鐘腳程。

Five minutes on foot.

屋內設備

▶開(燈)。

Turn on (the light).

▶關(燈)。

Turn off (the light).

└註：幾乎所有電器設備都可以用 turn on/off 來表示開/關。

▶將(音量)轉大

Turn up (the volume).

▶將(音量)轉小。

Turn down (the volume)

└註：只要有漸大漸小等調節功能的電器，幾乎都可以使用 turn up/down
來說明變大或變小。

▶鎖上門。

Lock the door.

▶開門鎖。

Unlock the door.
Open the door.

▶開(窗)。

Open (the window).

▶關(窗)。

Close (the window).
Shut (the window).

▶讓它開著/關著。

> Leave it open/closed.
> Leave it on/off.

> └ 註：on/off 指的是電器等的開啟或關閉。
> open/closed 則多指門窗類的打開或關起來。

▶有電話嗎？

> Is there a telephone?

▶電話響了。

> The telephone is ringing.

▶有熱水供應嗎？

> Is hot water available?

▶水一直在流

> Water is running.

▶(房間)有暖氣。

> There is a heater.
> There is a radiator.

▶有中央空調。

> There is central air-conditioning.

▶有網路。

> Internet is available.

▶將風扇打開/關上。

> Turn on/off the fan.

> └ 註：fan 泛指電扇、抽風機等電器。

住戶規定

▶禁止養寵物。

Pets are not allowed.

▶這不可以帶進(宿舍)來。

This is not allowed.

▶尊重你的鄰居(或室友)。

Be respectful to your neighbors.
Be respectful to your roommates.

▶請繳交管理費。

Please pay for the management fees.

關於室友或鄰居

▶我室友要開派對。

My roommate is throwing a party.

▶我室友老是在開派對。

My roommate is always partying.

▶我的樓友不在。

My flat mate is not home.

▶他是我的鄰居。

He is my neighbor.
He lives next door.

抱怨鄰居

▶我無法忍受這種吵鬧。

I can't stand the noise.

▶我鄰居快把我弄瘋了。

My neighbor is driving me crazy.

▶我快受不了這噪音了。

The noise is killing me.

▶我需要安靜一點的空間。

I need a quiet space.

▶對住戶委員會抱怨。

Complain to the residence association.

▶你有沒有跟鄰居溝通？

Did you speak to your neighbors?

▶沒有用。

It doesn't work.

└ 註：與鄰居溝通無效的意思。

▶我可以換房間嗎？

Can I change a room?

▶我可以跟你交換房間嗎？

Can I switch my room with you?

設備損壞 – 電器用品

▶燈壞掉了。

The light doesn't work.

▶燈泡燒壞了。

The bulb is burnt out.

▶日光燈一直在閃。

The tube is flickering.

▶我想我燒壞保險絲了。

I think I just blew the fuse.

▶燈泡壞掉了。

The bulb is dead.

▶燈絲斷了。

The filament broke.

▶空調壞了。

The air conditioner does not work.

▶電視不能看。

The TV doesn't work.

▶我的音響壞掉了。

My stereo is broken.

設備損壞 - 廁所

▶廁所堵住了。

The toilet is backed up.
The toilet is plugged up.
The toilet drain is clogged.

▶馬桶水不能沖了。

The toilet would not flush.

▶浴盆需要修理。

The bathtub needs repairing.

▶用馬桶吸盤。

Use the plumber's friend.
Use the plumber's helper.

▶排水管不通。

The drain is blocked.

▶用通水管的器具通一下。

Clear it with a drain auger.
Clear it with a pipe snake.

└ 註：一種長而有彈性的器具，用來塞入水管以取出堵塞物。

▶用吸盤疏通水管。

Clear the drain with a plunger.

└ 註：馬桶用吸盤也叫做 plunger。

▶試試看通樂。

Try drain cleaner.

└ 註：不嚴重的水管堵塞，一般家庭常使用通樂來清除水管內造成阻礙
的髒污。

▶水管通了。

It's cleared.

▶水管破了。

The pipe is broken.
The pipe is cracked.

▶水管要替換了。

The pipe needs to be replaced.

▶我們要找水管工人來。

We need to call a plumber.

▶沒有熱水。

There is no hot water.
There isn't any hot water.

▶熱水器/暖氣壞掉了。

The heater is out of order.

▶水滴得到處都是。

The water is dripping all over.

設備損壞－其他

▶這個東西壞掉了。

This is not working.

▶可以請你來修一下嗎？

Can you fix it, please?

▶我聞到瓦斯的味道。

I smell a gas leak.

▶電池沒電了。

The battery is dead.

停水/停電

▶是短路。

It's a short circuit.

▶跳電了。

The circuit breaker tripped.
The circuit breaker jumped.

▶停電了。

The power is cut off.
It's out of electricity.

▶造成停電的原因是什麼？

What causes the blackout?

▶一片黑暗。

It's complete darkness.

▶停水了。

We have no water.

We are out of water.

└ 註：out of XX 就是 XX 用完了的意思，XX 可以依照想表達的事物代換。

▶修好了。

It's back.

└ 註：停水或停電狀況修復後恢復供水/電。

做家事

▶我要打掃。

I have to clean up.

▶整理房間。

Clean up your room.

└ 註："clean up" 可用在表達 "整理或清潔" 的動作。

▶我在做家事。

I am doing house work.

▶拖地板

Mop the floor.

▶洗碗筷。

Do the dishes.

▶整理床鋪。

Make the bed.

▶擦拭窗戶。

Wipe the windows.
Clean the windows.

▶把你的房間整理乾淨！

Tidy up your room!
Clean up your room!

▶掃地。

Sweep the floor.

▶把地上的碎屑掃在一起。

Broom up the scraps.

▶倒垃圾。

Take out the trash.

▶清潔百葉窗。

Dust the blinds.

└註：撢灰塵的撢，動詞就用 dust。

▶吸地毯。

Vacuum the carpet.

▶把桌上的灰塵擦乾淨。

Wipe the table.
Dust off the table

▶把髒污擦掉。

Wipe out the stain.

▶擦鍵盤。

Swab the keyboard.

▶我要洗碗。

I need to do the dishes.

整理環境

▶除花園內的雜草。

Weed the garden.

▶剪草，除草。

Mow the lawn.
Cut the grass.
Get rid of the weeds.

▶耙樹葉雜草。

Rake the leaves.

▶為植物澆水。

Water the plants.

▶修剪枯萎的花朵。

Trim the faded flowers.
Shear the plant.

▶修剪樹木。

Cutting the tree.

▶為花園施肥。

Dunging the garden.
Fertilize the garden.

▶播種。

Seeding.

▶種花。

Plant flowers.
Grow flowers

▶種植物。

Raise plants.

▶種菜。

Grow vegetables.

▶他很擅長園藝。

He has a green thumb.

▶他在整理花園。

He is gardening.

房屋式樣

▶我租了一間獨棟房子。

I rent a house.

I rent a single house.

I rent a detached house.

└ 註：house 就是不與別人家相連，獨棟獨院的房子，通常有前院或後院。

▶我住在公寓裡。

I live in an apartment.

└ 註：在北美地區 apartment 多指出租公寓，大樓式住家的一個單位也叫做 apartment。不同地區的說法可能有些許差異。

▶我住在公寓裡。

I live in a flat.

└ 註：flat 也是公寓，不過通常指沒有電梯，大約 3-4 層樓高的公寓。

▶我有一間公寓。

I have a condo.

I have a condominium.

└ 註：condo 也是公寓。一般在北美地區 condo 指的是每戶產權獨立的公寓，住戶擁有房屋的所有權。而 apartment 則多指出租公寓。不同地區的說法可能有些許差異。

▶我住在合作公寓裡。

I live in a co-op.

I live in a corporative.

└ 註：co-op 跟 condo 雷同，不一樣的地方僅在於所有權細節。不同地區的說法可能有些許差異。

▶我住在連棟房屋中的一棟。

I live in a town house.

└ 註：town house 也是獨門獨戶的住宅，大約兩到三層樓左右。通常是一整排外觀一樣的房子連在一起，各自獨門獨戶。不同地區的說法可能有些許差異。

▶我有一幢雙併的透天厝。

I have a duplex house.
I have an attached house.
I have a semi-detached house.
I have a semi-attached house.

└ 註：只有一面牆壁跟鄰居相連的房子。

▶我有一台住房拖車。

I have a mobile home.
I have a trailer.

└ 註：顧名思義就是裡面有居家空間的車子，可以開在馬路上的房子。

▶我住在一幢別墅裡。

I stay in a villa.

▶這是一間小木屋。

This is a bungalow.

▶我住在帳篷裡。

I live in a tent.

其他

▶這是您的鑰匙。

Here is your room key.

▶我的鑰匙遺失了。

I lost my key.

▶請填一下這份表格。

Please fill out the form.

▶你準備住哪裡？

Where are you going to stay?
Where are you going to live?

▶這是私人產業。/這是私有住宅。

This is private property.

▶我在這裡租了一層公寓。

I rent an apartment here.

▶我住在這裡很久了。

I have lived here for a long time.

▶我以前住在那裡。

I lived there.

▶有我的信/留言嗎？

Any mail/message (for me)?

Chapter 7

聊天-行育樂

最常遇到的狀況與情境

指引方向用語

▶到 XX 怎麼走？

Which way is XX?

▶在樓上。

Upstairs.

▶在樓下。

Downstairs.

▶在你左手邊。/左轉。

On your left.
Turn left.
Take a left turn.
Make a left turn.

▶在你右手邊。/右轉。

On your right.
Turn right.
Take a right turn.
Make a right turn.

▶在你前面。

In front of you.

▶在你後面。

Behind you.

▶就在你旁邊。

Right beside you.

▶在這裡迴轉。

Make a U turn.

▶請跟著指標走。

Please follow the sign.

▶我找不到指標。

I can't find the sign.
I don't see any sign.
Where is the sign?

▶在紅綠燈那邊。

At the traffic light.

▶過了紅綠燈。

Pass the traffic light.

▶直走到底

Keep going.
Go straight.
Go straight down.
Go straight ahead.
Straight on.
Keep moving straight.
Continue straight.

▶就在對面而已。

Just across the street.

▶過這個十字路口。

Cross the intersection.

▶改變方向

Change direction.

▶下一個路口轉彎。

Turn at the next intersection.

▶後退。

Back up.

▶回頭。

Go back.

▶跟著我。

Follow me.

▶跟好。

Follow up.

▶在這兩棟建築物之間。

Between the two buildings.

▶在下一個紅綠燈(路口)。

At the next traffic light.

▶就在轉角附近而已。

Around the corner.

▶去那裏要花多久時間？

How long will it take?

▶第三條街之後。

In three blocks.
On the third corner.

▶到 XX 有多遠？

How far is it to XX?

▶有多遠？

How far away is it?

▶很遠嗎？

Is it far?

搭電梯

▶搭電扶梯。

Take the escalator.

└ 註：在英式及美式英語中 escalator 都是指電扶梯。

▶電梯向下。

The elevator is going down.

▶電梯向上。

The elevator is going up.

▶電梯停止了。

The elevator stopped.

└ 註：美式英文中的 elevator 指的是升降電梯，而在英式英文中則以 lift 表示。

►搭電梯。

Take the lift.

►搭電梯

Take the elevator.

►搭電梯下到 X 樓。

Take the elevator down to X floor.

►搭電梯上到 X 樓。

Take the elevator up to X floor.

迷路/問路

►我迷路了。

I'm lost.

►這是哪裡？

Where am I?
I need to know where I am.

►這條街叫什麼名字？

What street is this?

►查查地圖。

Check the map.

▶我需要一張地圖？

　　I need a map.

▶有沒有地圖？

　　Do you have a city map?

▶我在地圖上什麼地方啊？

　　Where am I on the map?

▶哪一邊朝上？

　　Which side up?

▶哪一邊是北邊？

　　Which way is north?

▶到博物館怎麼走？

　　Where is the Museum?
　　Which way is the Museum?
　　How to go to the Museum?

▶請你告訴我怎麼走？

　　Can you show me the way?

▶有明顯的路標嗎？

　　Are there any landmarks?

▶你有看到 XX 招牌嗎？

　　Do you see a sign that says XX?

騎腳踏車/機車

▶我想租一台腳踏車。

I'd like to rent a bike.

▶我要租一台機車。

I'd like to rent a scooter.

> 註：scooter 就是街上常見的小輪摩托車。至於 motorcycle 指的是有排檔的越野機車喔！

▶我有一台變速腳踏車。

I have a bike with gears.

▶我想買一台腳踏車。

I'd like to buy a bike.

▶我需要打氣筒。

I need a pump.

Do you have a pump for my bike?

▶我需要一個前燈。

I need a front headlight.

▶我要戴安全帽。

I need to wear a helmet.

▶把車上鎖。

Put a lock on my bike.

搭計程車

▶計程車！（伴隨招車動作）

Taxi!

▶你要去哪裡？

Where are you going?
Where would you like to go?

▶到博物館。

Museum, please.
To the Museum.
Take me to the Museum.

▶拜託開快一點。

Would you hurry, please?
Please hurry.

▶我趕時間。

I am in a hurry.
I am in a rush.

▶車資多少錢？

How much?
How much does it cost?
How much is the fare?
How much do I owe you?

▶我該給你多少小費？

How much should I tip you?

▶不用找錢。

Keep your change./Keep the change.

▶叫計程車。

Call a taxi./Call a cab./Grab a cab.

▶計程車招呼站在哪裡？

Where is the taxi stand?

▶這些幫我放到行李箱。

Put this in the trunk.

開車

▶我要租車。

I need a car.
I would like to rent a car.

▶請問您需要哪一款的車？

What kind of car would you like?

▶敞篷車要多少錢？

How much for a convertible?

▶我要一台新車。

I need a new car.

▶這是二手車。

This is a used car./This is second-hand.

▶這是我的駕照。

This is my driver's license.

▶這是我的國際駕照。

This is my international driver's license.

▶租金多少？

What is the rate?
How do you charge?

▶租金20元一天。

20 dollars for a day.

▶您要租多久？

How long will you need it?

▶我要租這台車一星期。

I'll take this for a week.

▶我要自排車。

I want an automatic car.

▶我要手排車。

I want a manual car.

▶這是按里程計費的。

It's charged by mileage.

▶有里程數限制嗎？

Is there a mileage limit?

▶(租車)沒有里程數限制

　　It's unlimited.

▶修車費多少錢？

　　What's the repair cost?

▶(幫汽車)做個全面檢查。

　　Take a diagnostic check.

▶沒有保險千萬不要開車。

　　Don't drive without insurance.

▶我有汽車貸款。

　　I have car loan.

▶保險會給付。

　　The insurance will cover.
　　The insurance will provide coverage.

▶這是禁止停車(違規拖吊)區。

　　This is the tow away zone.

▶不要超速。

　　Do not speed.

▶你會拿到罰單。

　　You will get a ticket.

▶塞車。

　　Traffic.
　　Traffic jam.
　　The traffic is heavy.

▶慢一點。

> Slower.
> Slow down.

▶快一點。

> Faster.
> Speed up.
> Accelerate.
> More gas.

▶停一下。等一下。

> Stay here.
> Stop here.

▶停車。

　路邊停車。

> Pull over.

▶並排停車。

> Double park.

▶我們會經過一個收費站。

> We'll go through a tollbooth.

▶我的車快要沒油了。

> No gas.
> I'm out of gas.
> I'm running out of gas.

▶加油站在哪裡啊？

> Where is the gas station?

▶請幫我加滿汽油。

Fill it up, please.

▶需要什麼油？

What do you need?
What kind of gas do you want?

▶請給我無鉛汽油。

Lead free gas.

▶請給我普通汽油。

Regular, please.

▶我的車就是發不動

My car won't start.

▶我們的汽車拋錨了。

We had a breakdown.

▶我們得找人過電發動。

We need to jump start our car.

▶我的車爆胎了

I got a flat tire.

▶你有備胎嗎？

Do you have a spare tire?

搭公車

▶我搭12路公車。

I take #12.

▶我該搭哪一路公車呢？

Which bus should I take?

▶這台公車有到博物館嗎？

Does the bus go to the Museum?

▶巴士車站在哪裡？

Where is the bus stop?

▶公共汽車票多少錢？

How much is the bus fare?

▶這是免費公車。

This is fare-free service.
This is free service.

▶恕不找零。

Exact change, please.

▶下一班巴士是什麼時候？

When is the next bus?
When does the next bus depart?

▶請提醒我什麼時候該下車。

Please tell me when to get off.

▶請提醒我該在哪裡下車。

Please tell me where to get off.

▶我應該在哪裡下車？

Where should I get off?

▶請讓我在這裡下車。

Please let me off here.
I need to get off here.

▶下一站。

Next stop.

▶要搭多久？

How long does it take?

▶我坐過站了嗎？

Have I passed the stop?

▶我要換車。

I need to change bus.

▶公車站在哪裡？

Where is the bus stop?

▶你應該在這裡等車。

You should wait at the bus stop.

▶我在這站下車。

This is my stop.

搭火車/地鐵/捷運

▶下一班車是幾點？

When is the next train?

▶最近的車站在哪裡？

Where is the nearest station?

▶下一站是哪一站？

What is the next station?

▶這班車是在哪一個月台？

What platform is this?

What platform does the train leave from?

▶我想訂個臥舖。

I need a berth

I need a roomette.

▶我要訂 XX(日期)的車票。

I need to get a ticket for XX.

I need to book a ticket for XX.

▶我們會在這站停留多久？

How long do we stop here?

▶我在中途可以下車嗎？

Can I stop over on the way?

└ 註：stop over 就是在途中下車遊覽甚至過夜，再搭下一班車繼續行程
的意思。

搭船

▶這艘渡輪在哪個碼頭上船？

What pier is the ferry?

▶船上有醫務室嗎？

Is there a clinic on boat?

▶船靠岸了。

The ship is in port.

▶我的船位在哪一層甲板？

What deck is my cabin?

▶這是我的艙位。

This is my cabin.

▶我要到上一層甲板。

I am going to the upper deck.

▶我們去休息室。

Let's go to the lounge.

VOCABULARY
相關單字

ship	船
jet boat	噴射艇

搭飛機

▶飛機準備起飛了。

The plane is taking off.

▶飛機在降落了。

The plane is landing

▶請繫好安全帶。

Fasten your seat belt.
Please keep your seat belt fastened.

▶把你的踏板放回原處。

Put your footrest back in place.

▶把你的桌子收回原處。

Put your tray back.
Lock your table in place.
Stow your tray table.

▶豎直椅背。

Put your seat up.
Upright your seat
Move your seat to the upright position.

▶安全帶燈號亮了。

The seat belt sign is on.

▶安全帶燈號滅了

The seat belt sign is off.

▶請回坐位。

Please return to your seat

▶請勿離座。

Please remain seated.

▶轉機櫃檯在哪裡？

Where is the connecting flight counter?

▶哪一班是我的轉機班機？

Which is my connecting flight?

▶我將在台北轉機。

I will transfer at Taipei airport.

▶我要換機去香港。

I am in transit to Hong Kong.

▶我們在這裏停留多久？

How long will we stop here?

▶請幫我辦登機手續。

Check in, please

▶這是我的登機證。

This is my boarding pass/card.

▶這是我的行李認領單。

This is my luggage claim slips.

▶登機門是幾號？

What is the gate number?

▶現在開始登機。

Boarding now.
Aboard.

▶歡迎登機。

Welcome aboard.

▶登機門要關了。

The gate is closing.

▶請拉開您的桌子。

Pull open your table.

▶何時用餐？

When will the meal be served?

▶洗手間在哪裡？

Where is the lavatory?

▶請幫我把它(外套)掛起來。

Could you hang this up?
Could you take this for me?

▶怎麼關掉/啟動這個？

How to turn this off/on?

▶我有一點暈機。

I feel sick.

▶可以給我一點熱水嗎？

Can I have some hot water, please?

詢問交通工具資訊

▶請問準點嗎？

Is it on schedule?

▶請給我一份時刻表

May I have a timetable?

▶出發時間是 XX。

The departure time is XX.

The time of departure is XX.

▶抵達時間是 XX。

The arrival time is XX.

The time of arrival is XX.

▶車/飛行時間是 XX。

The traveling time is XX.

The flight time is XX.

└ 註：flight 專指飛行時間。

▶時差是多少啊？

What is the time difference?

▶班機準時到達。

The flight arrives on time.

▶班機延遲了。

The flight is delayed.

買票/訂車(機)位

▶這是我的票。

This is my ticket.
This is my air ticket.

▶費用多少錢？

How much is the fare?
How much does it cost?

▶票有折扣嗎？

Is there any discount?

▶請給我往倫敦的票。

A ticket to London, please.

▶還有空位(可供訂位)。

There are openings.

▶請取出你的護照和機票。

Passport and ticket, please.

▶訂車/機位。

Book a ticket.
Make a reservation.

▶確認車/機位。

Re-confirm the ticket.

▶取消車/機票。

Cancel the ticket.

▶更改訂位。

Change the ticket.

▶來回票 。

Round-trip ticket.
Return ticket.

▶單程票。

One-way ticket.

▶這是你的行程。

This is your itinerary.

劃位

▶請給我靠窗的座位。

A window seat, please.

▶請給我靠走道的座位。

An aisle seat, please.

▶請給我中間的座位。

A middle seat, please.

▶緊急出口旁的位置。

The emergency exit seat.

▶我喜歡伸腳的空間大一點。

I like more legroom.

▶我坐經濟艙。

I take economy class.

▶我坐商務艙。

I take business class.

▶我坐頭等艙。

I take first class.

▶我想做機票升等。

I want to use the upgrade.

I want to upgrade my ticket.

座位

▶我朋友跟我的座位分開了。

My friend and I are split.

▶我可以換個位子嗎？

Can I change seat?

▶我想換到那個位子。

I'd like to move to that seats.

▶妳可以幫我們換一下位子嗎？

Can you change seats for us?

└註：請服務人員幫忙調動座位。

▶這位子有人。

The seat is taken.

▶我可以跟你換位子嗎？

Would you switch seats with me?
Can I switch my seat with you?

▶你坐了我的座位。

You are in my seat.

▶座位21A 在哪裡？

Where is 21A?

▶我的座位是21A。

I am in seat 21A.

寄送行李

▶辦行李託運。

Check the baggage.

▶將行李放在磅秤上。

Put baggage on the scale.

▶我有一樣隨身行李。

I have one carry-on item.

▶這個箱子太大了。

This case is too big.

▶這個箱子太重了。

This case is too heavy.

▶這不可以帶上(交通工具)。

This is not allowed.
You can't take it on board.

▶這是我的行李條。

This is my claim check.
This is my baggage slip.

▶到行李輸送帶領取行李。

Claim my baggage at the belt.

▶我能將手提行李放在這兒嗎？

Can I put my baggage here?

▶請幫我拿一下行李。

Please help me with my baggage.

└ 註：不管是要放到架子上，還是想拿下來都可以使用。

▶座位上頭放行李的櫃子。

The overhead luggage compartment.

▶我少了一箱行李。

I am missing one case.

VOCABULARY 相關單字

Cart	推行李的箱子
Lost luggage office	行李遺失申報處
Baggage claim area	行李提領區

過海關

▶請填表格。

Fill in the Form.

▶如何填寫這張表格？

How to fill in this form?

▶這是我的護照。

Here is my passport.

▶我沒有東西要申報。

I have nothing to declare.

▶請打開這件行李。

Please open this bag.

VOCABULARY
相關單字

Customs	海關
Tax	稅
Duty	稅
Duty-free	免稅
Exempt	免稅

行的目的

▶我來度假。

I am here on vacation.
I am here for sightseeing.

▶我來洽公。

I am here for business.
I am here for work.

▶我來移民。

I am applying for immigration.

▶我想移民到加拿大。

I am applying for Canadian citizenship.

▶我來唸書。

I am here to study.

▶我來拜訪朋友。

I am here to visit a friend.
I am here to see my friends.

▶我只是過境而已。

I'm just in-transit.
I'm just passing through.

其他

▶我要趕飛機(火車)。

I have a flight to catch.
I have a train to catch.

▶祝你旅途愉快！

Enjoy your trip!
Enjoy your journey!
Bon voyage!

▶我在途中。

I am on the way.

▶今天是國際無車日。

It's the International Car Free Day.

▶我經常騎腳踏車上班。

I usually bike to work.
I usually go to work by bicycle.

└ 註：bicycle=bike。

▶我是一個自行車迷。

I am a road-bike lover.

▶我走路來的。

I come here by foot.

育樂

玩樂

▶我們一起玩吧。

Let's hang out together.
Let's have fun together.
Let's go out together.

▶我知道一個好玩/很棒的地方。

I know a great place.

▶我們見個面喝一杯吧。

Let's meet for a drink.

▶玩拼字遊戲。

Play scrabble.

▶我大富翁。

Play monopoly.

▶玩橋牌。

Play bridge.

▶下西洋棋。

Play chess.

▶我們來玩躲貓貓(捉迷藏)。

Let's play catch.
Let's play hide and seek.
Let's play I spy.

▶我們來玩剪刀石頭布。

我們來猜拳。

Let's play rock-paper-scissors.

▶丟銅板吧。

Toss a coin.

▶正面還是反面？

Heads or tails?

▶誰當鬼？

Who will be it?

▶我當鬼。

I am the ghost/I am it.

▶Jimmy 當鬼(猜輸的人)。

Jimmy is the odd man out.

▶躲在衣櫥裡。

Hide in the closet.

▶你去躲起來吧。

You go hide.

▶數到二十。

Count to twenty.

▶我來(找你)囉！/你在哪兒啊？

Here I come!
Where are you?

▶找到你囉！

Here you are!
I found you!

▶我想玩盪鞦韆。

I want to play on the swing.

▶我們來玩翹翹板吧。

Let's play the seesaw.

▶我們來玩追人遊戲吧。

Let's play tag.

▶來追我啊！

Come get me!
Come catch me!

▶我們來玩球吧。

Let's play ball.

▶接住！

Catch!

▶我在鞦韆上。

I am on the swing.

▶我在木馬上。

I am on the rocking horse.

▶不給糖就搗蛋

Trick or treat.

▶我們來玩溜溜球。

Let's play yoyo.

▶我在溜滑梯上。

I am on the slide.

▶來玩井字遊戲吧。

Let's play tic tac toe.

└註：井字遊戲，就是劃一個井字，兩方各以圈或叉為記號，先連成一
　　線者為贏家。

▶玩拼圖。

Play a puzzle.
Solve a puzzle.
Let's do a puzzle.
Play jigsaw puzzle.

▶一片一片拼起來。

Put the pieces together.

▶玩填字遊戲。

Solve crossword puzzle.

▶你猜得出來那個字嗎？

Can you guess the word?

▶我解不出來。

I can't solve it.

▶看一下提示。

Just read the clue.

開派對

▶我要開個派對。

I am throwing a party.
I am organizing a party.

▶我們開個派對吧。

Let's have a party.
Let's throw a party.

▶這是個每人帶一道菜的派對。

It's a potluck party.

▶今晚來瘋狂一下吧。

Let's get crazy tonight.

▶我們開個睡衣派對吧。

Let's have a pajama party.

VOCABULARY
各種派對

Bachelorette party	單身女子派對		
New year's eve party	跨年派對		
Bachelor party	單身派對		
Wedding party	結婚派對	Kitchen shower	新居落成派對
Farewell party	歡送會	Costume party	化妝派對

參加社團

▶我有參加社團。

I joined a club.

▶我對網球社有興趣。

I am interested in the Tennis club.

▶你參加姊妹會/兄弟會。

I am in the sorority/fraternity.

▶我參加棒球校隊。

I joined the school baseball team.

看電影

▶我們去看電影吧。

Let's watch a movie.
Let's go to a movie.
Let's go see a movie.

▶我是一個電影狂。

I am a movie junkie.
I am really into movies.

▶我要看 XX(電影名)。

I want to see XX.

▶演員是誰？

Who is in the movie?

▶今晚演什麼？

　　What's on tonight?
　　What's playing tonight?

▶你想看什麼？

　　What movie do you want to see?
　　What would you like to see?

▶下一場幾點？

　　When is the next movie?

▶這電影有多長啊？

　　How long is the movie?

▶電影結束了。

　　The movie is over.

▶沒有座位了。

　　No seats left.

▶兩個後面一點的位子。

　　Two seats in the back.

▶我們到前面去坐吧。

　　Let's go sit in the front.

▶前面那個人擋住我了。

　　The guy is in my way.
　　The guy blocked my sight.

▶你介意跟我換一下位子嗎？

　　Would you switch seats with me?

▶我們買點爆米花

　　Let's get some popcorn.

▶這電影真好看。

　　This is a great movie.

▶這電影真難看。

　　This is a lousy movie.

　　The movie sucks.

▶這電影現在是部大熱門。

　　The movie is a big hit.

看戲/藝文表演

▶你要看那一齣？

　　Which play would you like to see?

▶劇院上演什麼呢？

　　What's playing in the theater?

▶我想看音樂劇。

　　I want to see a musical.

▶我想看歌劇。

　　I want to see an opera.

▶我今晚要去看演唱會。

　　I am going to a concert tonight.

▶我今晚去看了一場秀。

I went to a show tonight.
I went to see a show tonight.

▶給我一張節目單好嗎？

May I have the program?

▶這表演有多久？

How long is the play?

▶我朋友給了我一張票。

My friend gave me a ticket.

▶跟我一起去吧。

Would you go with me?

▶那裡可以買到門票？

Where can I buy a ticket?

▶那裡有售票亭。

There is a box office.
There is a ticket booth.

▶我們的票都賣光了。

We are sold out.

去酒吧

▶我知道一個不錯的酒吧。

I know a great pub.

▶我可以請你喝飲料嗎？

Can I buy you a drink?

Can I offer you a drink?

▶那位小姐請你喝飲料。

The lady over there offers you a drink.

▶她的下一杯飲料由我請。

Her next drink is on me.

▶我們一起出去喝個啤酒或什麼的。

Let's go out for a beer or something.

▶我請大家喝啤酒。

I am offering everyone a beer.

▶這一輪(飲料)我請客。

This round is on me.

▶下一輪(飲料)該我請。

I get the next round.

▶我們去玩遊戲桌吧。

Let's play some table game.

└ 註：pub 裡常見到一些手足球桌等等，就是遊戲桌。

去賭場

►我們去賭場玩吧。

Let's go to the casino.
Let's go risk some money.

►我們去試試手氣吧。

Let's go try some luck.

►我去了賭場。

I went to a casino.

►你要玩那一種？

What game would you like to play?

►請換籌碼。

Change, please.

►我想試試吃角子老虎。

I want to try the slot machine.

►我會在21點那邊。

I will be at the blackjack table.

►擲骰子吧。

Roll the dice.
Throw the dice.

►來玩撲克牌吧

Let's play cards!

▶一付牌

A deck of cards.
A pack of cards.

▶花色是梅花的牌。

The suit of clubs.

▶每種花色有14張牌。

There are 14 cards in each of four suits.

▶黑桃老 K。

The king of spades.

▶請不要作弊。

Please don't cheat.

▶我的牌面較大。

I have the higher card.
I have the higher poker hand.

▶我的牌面較小。

I have the lower hand.

▶我要試試運氣。

I am going to take the chance.

▶換牌。

Change cards.

▶丟牌。

Discard cards.

▶攤牌。

Show cards.

▶我有一付葫蘆。

I have a full house.

▶玩家贏。

The player wins.

▶莊家贏。

The dealer wins.

▶洗好牌了。

The deck is shuffled.

▶發牌。

Deal.
Deal card.
Deal with the cards.

▶該你發牌了。

It's your turn to deal the cards.

▶該你了。

It's your turn.
Your turn.

▶請等到下一輪吧。

Please wait for next spin.

▶請等下一輪。

Please wait for next roll.

▶請下注。

　　Please place your bet.
　　Place your chips.

▶賭大還是小？

　　Big or small?

▶我運氣真的太差了。

　　I am totally out of luck.

▶我贏到大獎囉。

　　I win the jackpot.

去運動

▶我們一起打 XX(運動)吧。

　　Let's play XX together.

▶我每天運動。

　　I work out everyday.
　　I exercise everyday.

▶你多久運動一次？

　　How often do you work out?

▶我經常運動。

　　I work out very often.

▶我去健身房運動。

　　I work out in a gym.

▶我每週去健身房兩次。

I go to the gym twice a week.

⌐ 註：去健身房(運動)就是 Go to a gym.

▶我經常去慢跑。

I usually go jogging.

▶我參加有氧舞蹈課。

I joined the aerobics class.

▶我每週都做階梯有氧。

I do step aerobics every week.

▶我們去跑一下跑步機吧。

Let's run on the treadmill.
Let's get a treadmill run.
Let's go for a run on the treadmill.

▶我們做點重量訓練吧。

Let's do some weightlifting.
Let's do some weight training.

▶我們去做仰臥起坐。

Let's do some sit-ups.

▶我們做伏地挺身吧。

Let's do push-ups.

▶運動前要先暖身。

Warm-up before work out.

▶一起吊一下單槓。

Let's do some chin-ups.

└ 註：正式名稱叫做引體向上。就是雙手拉單槓，將下巴抬到單槓上方。

▶我們去游泳吧。

Let's go swim.

▶我想去滑雪。

Let's go ski.
Let's go skiing.
Let's go snow surfing.
Let's go snow boarding.

看比賽

▶我們去看棒球賽吧！

Let's go to a baseball game!

▶這一場很精采的比賽。

This is a nice game.
This is a good match.

▶兩張主場比賽的票。

Two tickets for the home match.

▶這是一場客場比賽。

This is an away game.

└ 註：主場比賽就是 home match 或 home game。

▶那個隊伍是我們的主要對手。

That team is our major rival.

▶我們剛剛贏了。

We just won a match.

▶我們是排球校隊。

We are in the school volleyball team.

▶我們是地主隊。

We are the home team.

└註：guest team 就是客隊。

購物逛街

▶我想去跳蚤市場。

I want to go to the flea market.

▶只是看一看。

Just look around.

▶我們去逛街吧。

Let's go shopping.

▶我們去逛街吧！

Let's go window shopping!

└註：只逛街不購物就是 window shopping.

▶這在特價嗎？

Is this on sale?

▶這特價多久了？

How long has this been on sale?

▶特價有多久？

How long will the sale last?

▶貨比三家。

Shop around before buying.

▶一分錢，一分貨。

You get what you pay for.

▶這真是便宜。

This is a real bargain.

▶這很物超所值。

It's worth every penny.

▶我需要一件襯衫配我的裙子。

I need a shirt to go with my skirt.

▶這件我要了！

I will take it!

▶幫我包起來。

Wrap it up for me.

討價還價

▶多少錢？

　　How much is this?

▶你要出多少錢？

　　How much do you want?

▶便宜一點好嗎？

　　Cheaper?
　　Lower?
　　Can you offer a lower price?
　　Could you drop the price?
　　Can you give me a better price?

▶你可以賣最便宜多少錢？

　　What's your best offer?

▶我一次買兩個的話可以便宜一點嗎？

　　Do I get a better price for two items?

▶太貴了。

　　This is too expensive.

▶超出我的預算了。

　　This is beyond my budget.

給我打個折

▶給我一個折扣吧。

Give me a discount.

▶這是你給的最低價了嗎？

Is this your best offer?

▶算我便宜一點吧。

Give me a better deal.
Give me a cheaper price.

▶你能給的最低價是多少？

What's your best offer?

▶我可以討價還價嗎？

Can I bargain?
Is the price negotiable?

▶有打折嗎？

Is there any discount?

▶它不打折。

It's not on sale.
There is no discount.

▶我出10塊錢。

I give 10 dollars.

▶現金價打九五折。

5% discount for cash.

▶這是我的最底價了。

This is my final offer.

▶便宜一點我立刻買。

I'll buy it right away if it were cheaper.

▶你有沒有便宜一點的款式。

Do you have anything cheaper?
Do you have anything for less?

▶我們照標價賣。

The prices are fixed.

▶不能講價。

It's not negotiable.

▶我可以在其他地方問到更好的價錢。

I can get a better price at other places.

▶有折價券嗎？

Do you have any coupons?

▶已經很便宜了。

It's already a bargain.

▶不二價/不能討價還價。

No bargain.

▶她跟那個人討價還價。

She bargains with the guy over the price.

折扣標示

▶不二價

One price only.

▶免費

Free of charge.

▶這是特價品。

This is a special offer.

▶部分商品打85折。

15% off on selected items.

▶半價拍賣。

Half price sale.

▶憑此優待券優惠20%。
憑此優待券打八折。

20% off with this coupon.

▶買二送一。

Buy two get one free.

▶折價換新。

Trade in.

▶出清存貨

Clearance.

付款方式

▶我付現/刷卡。

I am paying in cash/credit card.

▶你們收不收信用卡？

Do you take credit card?

▶收不收旅行支票？

Do you take traveler's check?

▶只接受現金。

Cash only.

退貨

▶我要退貨。

I would like to return this.

▶我要換貨。

I want to replace this.
I want to exchange this.

▶我要退錢。

I want to refund this.
I'd like to get a refund.

▶有瑕疵。

This is defective.

▶這壞掉了。

這不能用。

> This is broken.
> This can't work.

▶這是我的發票。

> This is my receipt.
> This is my sales slip.

▶退款期限已經過了。

> The refund period is expired.

旅遊

▶我想安排一次旅遊。

> I want to arrange a trip.

▶你有沒有套裝行程？

> Do you offer package deals?
> Do you have package tours?

▶我要參加行程。

> I want to join the tour.

▶我要取消行程。

> I want to cancel the tour.

▶請安排當地地陪。

　　Please arrange a local guide.

▶導遊一天多少錢？

　　How much is a guide for a day?

▶五天的行程。

　　A five days trip.

▶我要四月一日出發的行程。

　　I'd like to leave on Apr 1.

▶我要四月十日回來的行程。

　　I'd like to return on Apr 10th.

▶我要城市導覽。

　　I would like a city tour.

▶我喜歡觀光行程。

　　I like to go sightseeing.

▶我喜歡購物行程。

　　I like to have a lot of shopping.

▶我要參觀所有的博物館。

　　I'd like to visit all the museums.

▶我想去美術館。

　　I'd like to go to the gallery.

▶所有行程全部包含在這個費用裡。

　　All activities are included in this charge.

▶附近哪裡好玩啊？

Where is the best spot in town?
What are the places of interest?

▶開放時間是幾點？

What's the opening hours?

照相

▶禁用閃光燈。

No flash.

▶禁止攝影。

No photographs.

▶照相。

Take a picture.
Take a photo.

▶幫我照相。

Take a picture for me.

203

▶按這裏就好了。

　　Just press here.

▶你介意讓我為你照張相嗎？

　　Do you mind letting me take a picture of you?

▶跟我一起照相好嗎?

　　Would you pose with me?

　　Take a picture with me, please.

▶請跟我一起照相吧。

　　Pose with me, please.

▶照張大合照吧。

　　Let's pose for a group picture.

▶以 XX (建築物或景物) 作為背景。

　　Get XX in the background.

▶從這個角度(照過去)。

　　From this angle.

▶我幫你拍張照。

　　Let me take your photo.

　　Let me take a shot of you.

▶一起照張相吧！

　　Picture time!

　　Let's take a shot!

　　Take a picture of us together.

▶設定(相機的)定時器。

Set up the timer.

▶準備好了嗎？

Ready?

▶別動！

Keep still!
Hold still!
Don't move!

▶笑一個！

Say cheese!

▶請笑笑。

Smile, please.

▶洗照片

Get this printed.

▶我要洗5X7的照片。

I want these in 5 inches.

▶你非常上相。

You look great on photos.

▶我會寄一張給你。

I will send you a copy.

▶我們多洗一套照片吧！

Let's print 2 copies!

Chapter 8

聊天-生活

遇到這些狀況時要會說

問天氣

▶外面的天氣如何?

What is it like out there?
How is the weather out there?

▶明天會下雨嗎?

Is it going to rain tomorrow?

▶今天天氣真好。

It's a beautiful day.
It's nice today.
It's sunny today.

▶只是在下毛毛雨而已。

It's just sprinkling
It's just drizzling.

▶大雨傾盆而下。

The rain poured down.
It rains pretty hard.
It's raining cats and dogs outside.

▶我們都溼透了。

We are all soaked.

▶天氣好熱。

It's so hot.
It's burning up out there.

└註:熱得跟火爐似的。

談情說愛

▶他們倆個有可能嗎？

Is it going to work out between them?

▶Mary 在跟 Joe 約會。

Mary is dating Joe.

▶我暗戀她。

I have feelings for her.
I have a crush on her.

▶她對他前男友還念念不忘。

She has not gotten over her ex.
She still can't forget her ex.
She still has feelings for her ex.

▶她已經忘了他了。

She is over him.

▶我們之間不可能有發展的。

Nothing will happen between us.

▶他們倆來電。

They were clicking.
They have chemistry.

▶他愛她。

He loves her.

貨幣兌換

▶請幫我換成美金。

Change this into dollars.

▶你要什麼面額？

What note do you want?
How would you like it?

▶兩張10元。

Two 10s.

▶請給我5元面額。

In fives, please.

▶匯率是多少？

What is the exchange rate?

▶請幫我換成零鈔。

Please break this.
Please break this into small change.

▶零錢。

Small change.
Small notes.

▶請幫我兌現。

Please cash this.

辦公會話

▶我想去拜訪你。

I would like to visit you.

▶我們定個約會吧。

Let's make an appointment.

Let's set up a meeting.

▶行程已經排定了。

The schedule is fixed.

▶我們約個時間吧。

Let's make an appointment.

▶安排星期四吧。

Make it Thursday.

▶晚上有時間嗎？

Are you free this evening?

▶我有空。

I am ok.

I am free.

I am available.

▶我連五分鐘都擠不出來。

I can't even squeeze 5 minutes.

▶我要接連開兩個會。

I have two meetings back to back.

另約時間

▶明天好嗎？

How about tomorrow?

▶大概什麼時候？

About when?

▶越快越好。

The sooner the better.

▶我看一下行程表。

Let me check my planner.
Let me check my schedule.

▶另外安排時間/延期。

Delay it.
Make it another time.

▶下午兩點怎樣？

Can you make it at 2pm?

▶長話短說！

Make it short!

▶我只有一小時的時間。

I only have an hour window.

▶會不會超過半小時？

Will it take longer then 30 mins?

物品代收/轉交/遞送

▶請把這個送到 XX 部門。

Please deliver this to XX.
Please send this to XX dept.

▶我會幫你轉交。

I will pass it for you.

▶我會幫你送過去。

I will drop it off for you.
I will send this over.

▶我會幫你拿回來。

I will get it back.

▶已經在送往 XX 的途中了。

It's on the way to XX.

▶我可以代收。

You can leave it with me.
Please leave it on my desk.

▶請幫我轉交給 XX。

Please pass it to XX.

└ 註：XX 用人名或職稱替代。

▶請務必告知他。/請確認他收到我的留言。

Please make sure he gets my message.

電腦壞了

▶我的電腦當掉了。

My PC is dead.
My PC got stuck.

▶電腦中毒。

It is virus.
I got virus.
My PC is infected.

▶重新啟動。

Reboot the system.
Reboot your PC.

請假

▶你該休一天假。

You should take a day off.

▶我要請一天假。

I need a day off.

▶我要請病假。

I'd like to take a sick leave.

▶我想請事假。

I'd like to take a personal leave.

▶他在休假中。

He is on leave.

▶他今天沒來。
　他今天請假。

> He is absent today.
> He took a leave of absence.

▶他去渡假了。

> He is on vacation.
> He is on holiday.

▶我今天可以早點離開嗎？

> Can I leave earlier today?

▶我覺得不舒服。

> I am not feeling well.

我要辭職

▶我要辭職。

> I quit.
> I resign.
> I'm quitting.
> I am leaving.

> └ 註：上述為較直接的說法。

▶我要辭職。

> It's time for me to leave.
> I would like to leave the job.
> I would like to resign.

> └ 註：上述為較委婉一點的說法。

辭職的原因

▶我想擴展我的視野。

I want to expand my vision.

▶我決定要出國念書了。

I decided to study abroad.

▶我需要好好休息。

I need to take a break.

▶我覺得無法勝任這個工作。

I am not up to this job.

職務代理

▶他是我的職務代理人。

He is my job substitution.

▶我會幫你代理一下工作。

I will cover for you.
I will watch your back.

休息時間

▶我要去吃飯了。

I am heading for lunch.

▶現在是休息時間。

It's coffee break.
It's lunch break.

▶休息一下喝杯咖啡吧。

Let's take a coffee break.
Let's take a break.

工作性質

▶我是半工半讀的學生。

I am a part-time student.

▶我兼職兩份工作。

I work on two jobs.

▶我有一份兼職工作。

I have a part time job.

▶我上夜班。

I work on the night shift.

文件審核

▶請過目一下這些文件。

Please look over these documents.

▶請在這裡簽名。

Sign here, please.

I need your signature here.

Please sign on the document.

▶請核准這份文件。

Please approve this document.

▶請共同核准這份文件。

Please co-sign this document.

▶請批准這份文件。

Please approve this document.

▶文件被退回來了。

The document was returned.

The document was sent back.

The document was turned down.

▶請你幫我看一下這份文件好嗎？

Would you check the document for me, please?

輪班班別

▶你連值兩個班。

> You work double shifts.
> You work two shifts.

▶我們換班。

> We trade shifts.
> We switch shifts.

▶你願不願意跟我換班。

> Would you switch shifts with me?
> Would you trade shifts with me?

工作內容

▶你的工作內容是什麼？

> What is your job description?
> What is your responsibility?

▶我負責的工作是 XX。

> I am working as a XX
> I am responsible for XX.
> I am in charge of XX.

> └ 註：XX 就是工作執掌的內容，可說出一或多項。

▶我有很多經驗。

> I have a lot of experiences.

▶我是一個XX。

I am working as a XX.

└註：XX 就是職位。

▶你從事什麼行業？

What line are you in?
What is your line?
What trade/profession are you of?

▶我在 XX 業。

I am in XX.
In the XX.

└註：XX 以行業別代入。

工作態度

▶我願意學習。

I am willing to learn.

▶我學的很快。

I am a fast learner.

▶她工作很有方法。

She works smart.

▶她很仔細。

She is thorough.

▶細心一點。

Be thorough.

交際邀約

▶我們希望邀請您們全體大駕光臨。

We would like to invite you all.

▶請參加我們的餐會。

Please join our party.

▶我想跟你見見面。

I'd like to meet you.
I'd like to see you.

▶這是您的邀請函。

Here is your invitation.

▶我會去。

I will be there.
Sounds great.
Meet you there!
I'll love to come.
I'll be delighted to come.

▶我不能去。

I am busy.
I can't make it.

▶我在忙別的事情。

I am tied up with something else.

開會英語

▶我們得開個會。

We should have a meeting.

▶我們開始囉？

Shall we start?

Let's get it started.

▶你們先開會吧。

不要等我了。

You go ahead first.

I will join you later.

I will catch up later.

Why don't you get started first?

Why don't you go ahead without me?

▶請注意。

Attention, please.

May I have your attention.

▶我們直接談到重點吧。

Let's cut to the point.

Let's get straight to the point.

▶你同意嗎？

Do you agree?

►同意。

I agree.
You are right.
I think this is very good.
So far so good.

►不同意。

I disagree.
This is not a good idea.
I don't think so.

►表示懷疑

Maybe.
I wonder.
I doubt it.
I am not sure.

└─註：提出懷疑，也可以表示不同意，較委婉的表達方式。

►有問題嗎？
　請提問。

Questions?
Any question?
Any comments?

►請幫忙把雷射筆遞給我。

Please pass me the laser pen.

►請幫忙關燈好嗎？

Would you get the light?

►請關閉百葉窗。

Shut the blinds, please.

展場接待

▶歡迎參觀我們的展示中心。

Welcome to our booth.
Welcome to our showroom.

▶我能為您服務嗎？

What can I do for you?
May I help you?

▶您需要找什麼嗎？

Are you looking for something?

▶請允許我帶你四處看看。

Let me show you around.
Please allow me to show you around.

▶下週即將推出。

It will come out next week.

▶這是我們的最新產品。

This is our new product.

▶這裡有免費樣品。

Here is some free samples.

▶這是我們的簡介/傳單/目錄。

This is our brochure/flyer/catalog.

Chapter 9

道別語

該說再見了

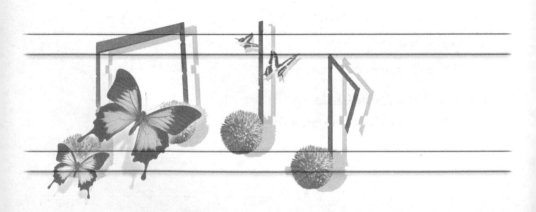

道別語

▶再見。

Good-bye.
I'll be seeing you.
Ciao!

└註：義大利語的再見。

▶謝謝您的來電。

Thanks for calling.

▶待會兒見！

Later!
See you around!
See you later!
See ya!

└註：See you 的簡說。

▶保重！

Take care!
Take care of yourself

▶該走了。

Gotta go.
Got to go.
Time to leave.
Time to go.

▶我該走了。

> I'd better go now.
> I have to go now.
> I should leave now.
> I got to be going now.

▶我正要離開。
　我很快就要走了。

> I am leaving.
> I am about to leave.
> Time to go.
> I must leave soon.
> I have to go in a few minutes.

└ 註：上述句子常用來當做脫身的藉口。

▶今天就到此為止吧。

> Let's call it a day.
> That's it for today.

▶我真的該走了。

> I really have to go.

▶我已經遲到了。

> I am already late.

└ 註：以上兩句表示非常急迫，必需離開。

▶我可以走了嗎？

> Can I leave now?

道別時的客套語

▶保持聯繫！

Keep in touch!

▶祝你有個美好的一天！

Have a nice day!

▶週末愉快。

Have a nice weekend!

▶祝你旅途平安！

Have a nice trip!

Have a nice flight!

　註：坐飛機旅行時用。

▶祝好運！

Good luck!

▶祝你玩的開心！

Have Fun!

▶改天再聚聚。

Let's get together again.

▶謝謝光臨。

Thank you all for coming.

▶今晚很愉快！

I had a wonderful evening!

▶很高興跟你談話。

Nice talking to you.

▶別忘了我們喔！

Don't forget us.

▶謝謝你的多方關照。
謝謝你為我所做的一切。

Thank you for everything.

▶我希望你在這裡時很愉快。

I hope you enjoyed your stay.

▶請代我向大衛問好。

Please say hello to David for me.

▶我很願意再跟你見面！

I'd love to meet you again!

└ 註：若對方開口邀約，而你也希望再次會面時的回答。

▶希望你今晚玩得開心。

I hope you enjoyed the evening.

└ 註：送女友回家時記得說這句話。

▶希望很快能再見到你。

I hope to see you soon.

▶上班/學校見囉！

See you at work/school!

用最簡單的英文來回答

本書除了集結食、衣、住、行、育、樂基本口語，亦囊括了情緒表達、醫療衛生、電話、及辦公室口語。一本書幫您行遍天下，用最簡單的英文句子，就可以清楚回答所有問題囉！Fill it up. 油箱加滿！The bulb is dead. 燈泡壞掉了。Who is in the movie? 演員有誰？I need a shampoo. 我要洗頭。Make it short! 長話短說！Give me a break. 饒了我吧！其實啊大家都把「說英文」想得太緊張囉！從耳朵接收到英語問句的那一秒鐘起，全身就繃了起來，一邊用力聽，一邊手忙腳亂地想：到底該怎麼回答…放輕鬆嘛！只要對口語熟悉一點其實最貼切的回答，往往是意想不到地簡單喔！

這就是你要的文法書

文法不是什麼大學問，說簡單一點，它不過就是英文字與英文字之間的一種組合規律。如果我們自小聽說讀寫都是靠著英語來溝通，對我們而言，可能沒有必要拿著一本文法書猛背，脫口而出的結果通常不會有太大的問題。這麼說是不是就不用學文法了呢？嗯…說實在話，這種想法有一點危險。中文與英文字的組合規則肯定是不同的，貿然的以中文邏輯結構成英文句子，不就成了所謂的「中式英語」(Chinese English)？在一般狀況下說 Chinese English，也許對方有些聽不懂，但依照當時情境以及說話者的身體語言，對方一定猜得出你的意思。可是，萬一是正式場合呢？比如：接待重要人物時，第一次跟老外主管見面時，或是任何一定要好好表現的重要場合，說中式英語立刻就有一種「遜掉了」的感覺。為了更完整正確的用英語表達，我們還是要學文法的。

ESI 英語現場調查：辦公室

藉由英語現場調查所提供的各種辦公室場景，幫助您建構一個學習英語的虛擬空間，讓您學得更快更印象深刻。在這個想像空間中，您的英語一定可以有長足的進步。從應徵面試、客戶關係的處理、任務指派、開會邀約、尋求援助，到秘書會話、電話英語、請假辭職、甚至是拒絕性騷擾，您在辦公室內可能見到的各種場景，盡在本書中一一呈現。藉著幾位固定主角在辦公室裡面發生的各種故事，架構出許多不同的場景。從應徵面試、工作期間各種狀況、客戶關係的處理、到秘書會話及電話英語、辭職，甚至是拒絕性騷擾都涵蓋在內了。

ESI 英語現場調查：遊學

什麼是 meal plan？住校，原來還有那麼多選擇啊？自己在外租屋要留意什麼事情？買車，什麼是該注意的？不買車的話，又該怎麼解決交通問題？還有最現實又最重要的成績，怎麼準備考試和報告，才能達到最高的讀書效率？這是一本專為夢想出國唸書、體驗真正遊學生活的人所設計的工具書。出國遊學，小 Case! 買張機票，Let's Go!

這就是你要的單字書

世界上最齊全的單字書當然是字典啦！可是，學單字總不能抱著字典從 A 背到 Z 吧，第二頁背完了，大概第一頁也忘得差不多了。本書依各種情境將單字分門別類，順著目錄翻下去，不但可以很快找到您要用的單字，還可以順便將相關的單字瀏覽一遍。這是一本最實用的英語單字書，從日常生活、吃喝玩樂，到美容保養，身體醫療，還有商業用字、求職面試、口語溝通、報刊新聞等等，內容包羅萬象。

你也能看懂運動英語

愛運動的你，可以經由本書將英語學習融入生活中。不懂運動的你，也可以從這裡開始入門。Come on！一起愛上運動吧！與國際足球粉絲們暢快地聊天，但說到重點處卻詞窮了，無法盡興表達嗎？和客戶一起去打高爾夫，可是除了離不開的生意經，還有沒有其他的話題呢？想第一時間知道大聯盟最新戰績，卻被外國網站上一大堆縮寫攪得迷迷糊糊嗎？花大錢買了國外運動雜誌想了解最新的 NBA 戰績評論，卻對上頭的術語一知半解嗎？這裡不但有體育頻道上常見的運動項目，還詳細解釋了重點規則及術語喔！幫助您看球賽學英文，順便和客戶搏感情！

商業實用英文 E-mail 業務篇(50 開)

最權威、最具說服力的商用英文 E-mail 書信，馬上搶救職場上的英文書信寫作。史上最強的商用英文 E-mail！三大特色：1000 句商用英文 E-mail+例句 500 個商用英文 E-mail 關鍵單字+33 篇商用英文 E-mail 範例。三大保證：輕鬆寫一封商用英文 E-mail+解決所有商用英文 E-mail+快速查詢商用英文 E-mail。三大機會：成功升遷+成功創造業務佳績+成功開創事業新契機。最搶手的商用英文寶典，提升實力就從「商業實用英文 E-mail（業務篇）」開始。

求職面試必備英文 附 MP3(50 開)

六大步驟，讓你英文求職高人一等馬上搶救職場的英文面試全國第一本針對「應徵面試」的英文全集！三大特色：三大保證：三大機會：成功升遷成功覓得新工作成功開創海外事業新契機學習英文最快的工具書，利用「情境式對話」，讓您英文會話能力突飛猛進！

Good morning 很生活的英語(50 開)

超實用超廣泛超好記好背、好學、生活化，最能讓你朗朗上口的英語。日常生活中，人們要透過互相問候來保持一種良好的社會關係。試想，早晨起來，風和日麗，吹著口哨去上學或上班，你的朋友從你對面走來卻沒有跟你打招呼說一聲「你好！」，你的感覺將會怎麼樣呢？你會不會覺得今天真是糟糕透了？心想：怎麼會這個樣子呢？因此，只要一聲 Good morning, Hello, Hi!不但拉近你和朋友的距離，更能為自己的人際關係加分。英語不能死背，用生活化的方式學英語，才能克服開不了口的窘境！套裝學習，一次 OK！

超簡單的旅遊英語 (附 MP3)(50 開)

出國再也不必比手劃腳，出國再也不怕鴨子聽雷簡單一句話，勝過背卻派不上用場的單字，適用於所有在國外旅遊的對話情境。

出國前記得一定要帶的東西：*護照*旅費*個人物品*超簡單的旅遊英語適用範圍*出國旅遊*自助旅行*出國出差*短期遊學…

單字急救包(48 開)

您可以塞在袋裡，放在車上，或是擺在角落不管是等公車的通勤族，還是上廁所前培養情緒隨手抽出本書，就可以利用瑣碎的時間充實一下，小小一本，大大好用喔！我們有最完整的單字內容，最便利的攜帶方式另外也提供您最簡便的查詢介面，從頁面側邊即可找出您需要的單字您不需要騰出大把的時間坐下來讀英文就讓語言能力在無形的中進步吧！

雅典文化

永續編號	書　　名	定價	作者

現代親子系列

永續編號	書名	定價	作者
S1405	如何跟你的小孩溝通	180	安娜・Chin
S1406	我教女兒學數學	280	獨狼
S1407	孩子畢竟是孩子	190	安娜・Chin
S1408	孩子，你真的好棒	190	方舟
S1409	父母是孩子的第一任導師	190	方舟
S1410	孩子不會永遠是孩子	190	方舟
S1411	寶寶睡眠聖經	299	蒂妮荷兒

另類學習系列

永續編號	書名	定價	作者
S1904	我的菜英文—菲傭溝通篇	180	張瑜凌
S1905	我的菜英文—運將大哥篇	180	張瑜凌
S1906	我的菜英文—旅遊篇	180	張瑜凌
S1907	我的菜英文【單字篇】	180	張瑜凌

HERO 系列

永續編號	書名	定價	作者
S2101	諾曼第大空降	380	Stephen E. Ambrose
S2102	我的FBI・黑手黨・柯林頓・反恐戰爭	399	路易士・弗利

生活英語系列

實用會話系列

實用文法系列

雅典文化

英語隨身系列

S3701 E-MAIL 業務英文隨身書	99	張瑜凌
S3702 菜英文隨身書-生活應用篇	99	張瑜凌
S3703 E-MAIL 秘書英文隨身書	99	張瑜凌
S3704 英語求職技巧隨身書	99	張瑜凌
S3705 E-MAIL 談判英文隨身書	99	張瑜凌
S3706 菜英文隨身書-運將篇	99	張瑜凌

英語工具書系列

S3801 你最實用的商業英文 E-MAIL	220	陳久娟
S3802 火星英文即時通	200	Joanne C.
S3803 用最簡單的英文來回答	200	Joanne C.
S3804 最簡單的英文自我介紹(附 MP3)	250	陳久娟
S3901 ESI 英語現場調查：辦公室	220	Joanne C.
S3902 ESI 英語現場調查：遊學	220	Joanne C.
S3903 你也能看懂運動英語	220	Joanne C.

英語 DIY 系列

S4101 這就是你要的文法書	220	陳久娟
S4102 這就是你要的單字書	220	陳久娟

ⓐ 雅典文化 讀者回函卡

謝謝您購買這本書。

為加強對讀者的服務，請您詳細填寫本卡，寄回**雅典文化**；並請務必留下您的E-mail帳號，我們會主動將最近"好康"的促銷活動告訴您，保證值回票價。

書　　名：用你會的單字說英文

購買書店：＿＿＿＿＿市／縣＿＿＿＿＿＿＿＿書店

姓　　名：＿＿＿＿＿＿＿＿＿　生　日：＿＿年＿＿月＿＿日

身分證字號：＿＿＿＿＿＿＿＿＿＿＿＿＿＿＿＿＿＿

電　　話：(私)＿＿＿＿(公)＿＿＿＿(手機)＿＿＿＿＿＿＿

地　　址：□□□＿＿＿＿＿＿＿＿＿＿＿＿＿＿＿＿

E - mail：＿＿＿＿＿＿＿＿＿＿＿＿＿＿＿＿＿＿

年　　齡：□20歲以下　　□21歲～30歲　□31歲～40歲
　　　　　□41歲～50歲　□51歲以上

性　　別：□男　□女　　婚姻：□單身　□已婚

職　　業：□學生　　　□大眾傳播　□自由業　□資訊業
　　　　　□金融業　　□銷售業　　□服務業　□教職
　　　　　□軍警　　　□製造業　　□公職　　□其他

教育程度：□高中以下（含高中）□大專　□研究所以上

職 位 別：□負責人　□高階主管　□中級主管
　　　　　□一般職員□專業人員

職 務 別：□管理　　□行銷　□創意　□人事、行政
　　　　　□財務、法務　　□生產　□工程　□其他＿＿＿＿

您從何得知本書消息？
　　　　□逛書店　　□報紙廣告　□親友介紹
　　　　□出版書訊　□廣告信函　□廣播節目
　　　　□電視節目　□銷售人員推薦
　　　　□其他＿＿＿＿＿＿＿＿＿＿＿＿＿＿＿

您通常以何種方式購書？
　　　　□逛書店　　□劃撥郵購　□電話訂購　□傳真訂購　□信用卡
　　　　□團體訂購　□網路書店　□其他＿＿＿＿＿＿＿＿＿＿

看完本書後，您喜歡本書的理由？
　　　　□內容符合期待　□文筆流暢　□具實用性　□插圖生動
　　　　□版面、字體安排適當　　□內容充實
　　　　□其他＿＿＿＿＿＿＿＿＿＿＿＿＿＿＿

看完本書後，您不喜歡本書的理由？
　　　　□內容不符合期待　□文筆欠佳　　□內容平平
　　　　□版面、圖片、字體不適合閱讀　□觀念保守
　　　　□其他＿＿＿＿＿＿＿＿＿＿＿＿＿＿＿

您的建議：
＿＿＿＿＿＿＿＿＿＿＿＿＿＿＿＿＿＿＿＿＿＿＿
＿＿＿＿＿＿＿＿＿＿＿＿＿＿＿＿＿＿＿＿＿＿＿

請下後青寄司「21台北系夕北市大同路3段14號9樓之1雅典文化效

2 2 1 0 3

台北縣汐止市大同路三段 194 號 9 樓之 1

雅典文化事業有限公司

編輯部　收

請沿此虛線對折免貼郵票，以膠帶黏貼後寄回，謝謝！

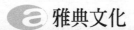

為你開啟知識之殿堂